INNES DOES MEXICO

INNES does Mexico
Allan F. Brack

Published by - Spines
ISBN: 979-8-89569-225-7

INNES does Mexico

Allan F Brack

Cast of Characters:

Duncan Innes - Federal Reserve in-house investigator

Marlee Johansen - Girlfriend of Duncan Innes living in Cape Town, South Africa

Mr. Assisi - Iranian Agent

Alan MacDonald - Federal Reserve head of security

Chairman DeVilliers - Bank of South Africa Chairman

D.E.A. Agents: Jose Fernandez, Josh Halpern

El Guapo Cartel:

Luis Alessandro Garcia - El Guapo (The Handsome One) himself, head of Cartel

Eddie Haddad - Iranian Infiltrator

Mohammed Saleem - Iranian Infiltrator

Casey O'Brien - Washington D.C. Police and former Innes girlfriend

Alfred Johnson - Envelope man, student agitator

President Evans - USA President and friend of Alan Macdonald

Secret Service Agents - Pete Gonzales and Harry Carlson

BND Agents:
   Hans Richter and Frederick Dietrich, Johann Pfaff
   Otto Sternberg - Head of Security Deutsche Bank Frankfurt
   Iranian Agents USA - Mr. Hassoon, Mr. Assisi

SOUTH AFRICA

The Falcon Jet announced its landing intentions at D.F. Milan Airport in Cape Town. At fifteen thousand feet, the pilot began his descent. Pulling back on the throttle, he was happy this trip was now over. The flight had originated in Kuwait and was expected to be on the ground for one day and then the turnaround back. The crew would be exhausted. It couldn't be helped, the owner wanted a short trip and it was his money. At three thousand feet, the pilot deployed full flaps and continued his descent. The airport was in sight. The sound of engines powering down could be heard throughout the plane. Passengers were now pulling their carry-ons together. Customs had been completed in Johannesburg, now it was a simple matter of reaching the gate and discharging his passengers.

At the gate, they were met by airport staff. The plane's hatch was opened and passengers were disgorged. Two were arguing loudly about where the first stop should be. The ramp personnel got out of the way letting the four passengers disembark. They all continued on through the Airport to the waiting limo at the arrivals point. Each piling through the open door held by the chauffeur. Assisi went in first. This was not his first trip to Cape Town.

"The bank, please, driver."

The limo sped away from the Airport entrance heading into the city. Table Mountain loomed to their left with the famous table-cloth spilling over its top.

One of the men commented on it. " That is really quite beautiful."

"Yes it is", said Assisi, " but we are not here to sightsee. At the bank, I will handle all of the wire transfer requests. You three, please stay outside and ensure I am not disturbed." At the bank, all three took up positions near the entrance and scanned the passerbys looking for threats.

Chairman DeVilliers met Assisi at the main entrance.

"Nice to see you again, Mr. Assisi. What can I do for you today?"

"Just a few wire transfers per our agreement."

"Yes, sir, quite happy to be of service. Please come into my office, which will be a little more private." DeVilliers led the way. Marlee watched him walk by her area. Assisi did not look at her. She immediately got on the phone and called Duncan.

"Guess who just walked into the bank?"

Duncan responded with, "Who?"

"Mr. Assisi, he is in with DeVilliers right now. He wants more wire transfers. Do you want them, or can we lay that all to rest?"

"Yes, I want them, however, only if no one sees you doing this. Stay safe, Assisi is not a good guy."

"When will you get back to the Condo? I miss you." Said Duncan.

"I'll be here another three hours and then come home. Stay out of trouble while I am gone, and put a bottle of Sauvignon Blanc in the Fridge."

'Yes, Maam. I'm on my way to the kitchen as we speak. Do you want to go out for dinner tonight or stay at home and order in?'

"Let's go out. There is a good Indian restaurant in Rosebank I want to try. Everyone says it is great and reasonable. In today's world, reasonable and great do not go hand in hand."

"Sounds good; I'll be waiting. Drive safely."
"There is another way?"

Cape Town

Duncan fired off an email to his boss, Alan MacDonald. Alan was the head of security now at the Federal Reserve. Duncan acted as his outside fixer and investigator. After the problems with Kuwaiti transfers the previous 12 months, Duncan had taken one month off in South Africa with his new Lady friend. Marlee was also employed by the South African Bank, which fed him with information on wire transfers that would otherwise have been unavailable to them. Duncan had been able to track down suspect wire transfers this way, making her a valuable asset. He still hated putting her in this compromising position.

Since three hours were available, Duncan decided to go out on his five-mile run. His daily routine required a minimum of three miles and weight room work. Cardio was important, but overall muscle tone was also a priority. Running was also a good time to review any open issues in his mind or activities he needed to prioritize. Putting Marlee in a compromising position was not something he enjoyed doing. He would be back at the Condo by the time Marlee returned home. Dinner at an Indian Restaurant sounded good, but they were usually a hit-or-miss proposition. His run was good, a bit slow, but he had taken a few days off his normal routine. The discipline needed to stay in top shape was exhaustive but worth the effort. The weather remained clear, if a little breezy. As usual, Duncan scanned the area through which he ran, looking for anything that might develop into a threat. Just last year, he had run into two thugs near Sea Point, putting them both in the Hospital for extended care. Keeping a low profile in his line of work as an investigator required him to keep off the local's radar as much as possible. Marlee ensured acceptance in the building, but that could easily change if local officials became aware of his existence. He decided to put in a call to Otto Sternberg in Germany.

The secretary of Otto put him straight through.

"Hi, Duncan; how are things in Cape Town?"

"All is well, and I thank you again for the introduction to Marlee."

"No thank you necessary, what's up?"

"Assisi is here in Cape Town again."

"That doesn't sound good. More wire transfers?"

"Yes, I should have copies tonight of what he is sending. I'll pass them through to you."

"Good. I think it is rapidly becoming time to shut this guy down. It's bad enough that he threw one of his men off the roof in Friedberg the last time he was in Germany. He is financing something. Maybe the wires will give us a clue."

"After I send them to you, I'll call again, and we can see how this affects your bank and mine. Do you still have a contact at the Bank of England?"

"Yes, not as good as Levick from our last little adventure but progressing with a new person. I'll tell you more about it when we see the wires."

"Thanks, Otto. Alan will be pleased. We still owe you from the last disaster."

"You do not owe me anything and that includes Marlee. How is she, by the way?"

"She is Doing very well. When Van Der Merve died, she was promoted to his job, and she is well respected in the bank."

"I'm glad to hear it. Be careful, Duncan. In our jobs, close personal relationships are rare, and they tend not to last when they are acquired."

"Understood, Otto, but I can't give her up now. It is all too good."

They agreed to speak once the copies of the wire transfers were available. Duncan decided on a shower before Marlee came back and checked his emails. The Inbox was empty, which normally was a good thing. If Alan was looking for him it meant there were a problems somewhere. That entailed travel to wherever he was needed. He was not prepared to give up Marlee just yet. Work would rear its ugly head very shortly when he got a look at the Wires. They both knew that his job required travel and rarely with more than a moment's notice. If he did have to leave, they were prepared for that eventuality. Duncan put the T.V. on knowing it would be mostly drivel. This time the newsreader gushed about how South Africa had tried to move against Israel in the World Court. The constant bombardment and attacks on Gaza were starting to wear thin. Israel was losing the P.R. war. From day one of the original Hamas attacks, Israel should have mounted a major P.R. campaign, which she did not do. The results were predictable. Even with all of the death and destruction and ongoing operations in Gaza, Israel was doomed to lose the hearts and minds of the World. Too many deaths for too little gain. The U.S. students were creating havoc in the streets of New York and other major metropolitan areas. Of course, if Mexico was bombing California to get their old areas back everyone would be outraged. When Hamas did it, it was the poor Palestinians. 'From the River to the Sea' rang quite hollow but made good television. That most students had no idea what they were chanting for or proposing was a minor detail. Commentators in South Africa felt Israel was over reacting and should be somehow curtailed. After ten minutes of this nonsense, Duncan changed the channel and was rewarded with an animal show on crocodile issues in Zambia. The Arab world had been beating this drum of anti-Israeli rhetoric for years. Everyone remembered the camps in Lebanon and Jordan, amongst others; no one wanted a repeat with refugee camps on its borders. Egypt was now in the same position and did not want to give up the Sinai to Palestinians and worry about them trying to overthrow the Egyptian government again. Rather, they felt leave it to the Israelis. Maybe they would come up with a solution to the masses of Palestinians now on the Egyptian border. Everyone knew a two-state solution was never going to fly. No one wants these people on their borders and a hotbed of future terrorists destabilizing the entire Middle East. The Israelis were never going to accept these people lining their borders. The sooner the World recognized this, the better for all concerned. The irony of the Holocaust and the destruction of Gaza was not lost on all. Now the rest of the Arab world would be under pressure to solve the unsolvable. The Americans paid lip service to the two-state solution. Yet any assurance they offered a future country of Palestine was unlikely to be believed. The country of the USA was no longer credible in any of its promises. The Ukraine had learned this lesson as had Afghanistan, Syria, and soon Taiwan would learn the hard way. America could only be trusted for one quarter of a year going forward. The political exigencies of the quarter would always take precedence. No American politician ever decided on what was right in the long run, only on what kept them in power. That could be taken to the bank at any time. Look at what appeared good in the short run and the Americans would always pick that option. That simple fact allowed China to become as powerful as she was and control significant portions of the world's industrial capability and manufacturing. The Americans had abdicated their enviable position in the world for short-term profits. Now, even their weapons were made in China, along with drugs, clothing, and other essential goods. Made Rome look understandable when the empire collapsed. Short-term was not Duncan's problem. Now that Assisi was back, he knew he would have to take that issue on again. Assisi was the bad penny that just kept coming up again and again.

"Honey, I am home. I thought I would use your phrase."

"Always a pleasure, Marlee. I do enjoy seeing you, especially when you come home." He reached out for her, pulling her in close. The smell of her hair and perfume was always was a cause of arousal.

"Happy to see me, I see!" she laughed.

"Indeed, tell me about the day at the bank."

"Everything was normal until Assisi tuned up. The chairman took him into his office and came out later with three wire transfers. I have copies for you in my bag."

"I hope no one saw you make copies."

"No, nothing looked out of the usual. We always make a few copies for the Bank records, for the wire people to act on, and, of course, a set for me. All good. Besides which, Assisi had already left, so he wouldn't have seen anything."

"What about your boss?"

"No, he left early but did ask me to expedite the wire transfers. It took about five minutes from the receipt of the wire requests to sending them out. The total amount was only 20 million—small transactions for the Kuwaitis. I checked to see if the money was in the Kuwaiti account, and it was; it came in yesterday."

"Okay, where did they go?"

"That is the odd part. At least one transfer was weird. Duncan, two went to London for forward transfer to Greece and Germany. That last one went to London as well for forwarding to Mexico. Here are the copies."

Duncan spread them out on the coffee table and photographed each page. These he would send to his boss in the USA, Alan MacDonald. One new headache was coming up via email. In some ways, Germany made sense, for there were many mosques in Germany with the resultant high Islamic population. They were mostly Turks, but some other Middle Easterners as well. Greece was a bigger question, and, of course, Mexico was the biggest one. These three transfers would give Alan something to do.

That evening, Marlee and Duncan were seated at a secluded table toward the rear of the Indian restaurant. The smell of the Indian spices and, of course, Marsala permeated the entire room.

There were only a handful of people being served. The food was good, if a bit spicy.

"I have wanted to come here for some time, Duncan. Everyone says it is great."

"I have to agree, but what my bowels will think of it in a few hours remains to be seen. 'Delhi Belly' did not come about without cause."

"Don't worry; you will be fine. I know of at least five people that come here on a regular basis and to date no complaints." She smiled as she said this.

"Well, as long as we do not make a habit of this place, it's fine." Duncan was not sure that "fine" was the right word. Everyone in the restaurant looked suspiciously thin. They finished up, paid the bill, and left the restaurant none the worse for wear. The ride back to Disa Park only took 25 minutes. Traffic was light. The view over Cape Town Harbor remained outstanding as they entered Marlee's flat. Duncan went to the sofa, sat down, and began to savor the vista that had opened up before him. Lights blinked throughout the city as far away as Blouburg Strand. This was a view that he would never get used to; everything was almost too perfect.

"Would you like a glass of wine?"

"Of course, please."

TRAVEL PLANS

The phone rang shortly after his return from a run to Camps Bay the next morning.

"Hi, Duncan. Thanks for the wire transfer copies. You have indeed opened another can of worms. The BND, as you know, is responsible for all intelligence received from home and abroad in Germany and is very excited. I took the liberty of copying one of my contacts there on the wire coming to Germany. They would have seen it anyway, but this way, they get a jump on the transfer." Otto paused to allow Duncan to respond.

"No problem, Otto. You do what you have to do. Keeping them on your side is important. One never knows when the BND (Bundes Nachrichten Dienst) will become helpful going forward."

"Agreed, the transfer was for a known Hamas front group that makes purchases in Europe for Gaza. Everyone is now going to be interested in how this money is spent."

"You will understand that this same information is now with Alan MacDonald?"

"I expected that, and the BND knows it as well."

"I expect to hear from Alan shortly. I will keep you informed."

"Thanks, Duncan. Same here."

"Talk to you soon. Keep out of the rain, Otto."

"Come on, it's not that bad here, even though Frankfurt does have that grayish reputation."

The call had been prophetic, as Alan MacDonald called almost immediately after Duncan had terminated the call to Otto in Germany.

"Hi, Duncan." Alan MacDonald sounded happy.

"Hi yourself. I assume you received the copies of the wire transfers."

"I did indeed, and thank you. We have already followed up on the German one, which seems innocuous. It appears just to be a support payment for the Mosque in Berlin. The amount the Mosque received was only three million, which is not unusual for them; it has happened before. An additional two million went to a Frankfurt Mosque. Also, it's not an unusual transfer per se but it appears harmless. It would seem, according to the BND, that the money is for renovations and enlargement of the mosque itself." That leaves fifteen million to run down. Early indications are five million for Greece, which is actually to be used by Hamas for medical, food, etc., for Gaza. I am still checking through Mossad how true this is. More when I have it."

"Okay, but what do you want me to do?"

"Right now, sit tight. I have a meeting scheduled with the President tomorrow. You can expect to hear from me after that meeting. In the meantime, enjoy your short-lived vacation."

"Thanks, Alan. Hopefully, nothing major will break, but I do smell a rat."

"As do I. Talk soon."

There was now nothing to do but wait. Marlee would be home later in the day. Duncan decided the best he could do would be to contact Otto again and see if the Germans knew something, but he doubted it. The Mexico connection was now more interesting. Alan would probably be able to run that one down. Greece would be addressed by the Mossad (Israeli intelligence) if and when they had time. That might take half a day or six months.

That evening, when Marlee came home, they decided to remain

in the flat. Marlee was an excellent cook, and there was lamb on the menu. The bank had been quiet that day, with no new visitors. The wire transfers were complete and acknowledged. Now all Duncan could do was wait for Alan or Otto to come back with something new. Duncan hated to wait, preferring action over idling. But if he had to idle, then being with Marlee was the way to do it. In the interim, he had checked on Casey, a past girlfriend, who was doing very well. She remained antsy that she was apartment-ridden to recover but relatively pain-free. After a great dinner, Marlee and Duncan once again repaired to the sofa, glasses of wine in hand.

"Duncan, how about a trip to Stellenbosch this weekend? I can show you the family winery in Paarl and you can meet some of my friends."

"Sounds good to me. Is this a day trip, or are we staying there overnight?"

"It's not far away, maybe an hour or two, so we can come back in the evening. Does Saturday work for you?"

"Marlee, whatever you want. I am happy to go there. Will there be more wine, like this one?" He held his glass up toward her.

"Absolutely. You will enjoy it. Paarl is beautiful, and the surrounding mountains."

"Then, I shall look forward to the trip."

Again, they returned to the bedroom. His comment that they were headed for another "slap and tickle session" brought a hefty response from Marlee.

"I slap, you tickle, Mr. Innes." He laughed, and they got up to go back to the bedroom a lovely habit.

Marlee's day started early the following morning. She had a number of meetings at the bank that could not be put off. She said her goodbyes and left the flat at eight a.m. Duncan was left to his exercise routine and run to Camps Bay again.

Alan called again late afternoon Duncan's cell phone.

"How are you doing today, Duncan?"

"Fine, how did the meeting with the President go?"

"He is very concerned about the recent transfers, in particular to

Mexico. The Greek one has been confirmed by Mossad; they know about the purchases by Hamas, nothing to be too concerned about there. The money is being spent on food and medical supplies. I did track down Assisi's flight plan and trip back to Kuwait. The bad news is he was not one of the passengers who got off the plane in Kuwait. That raises the question of where the hell he is. And, of course, what is he up to?"

"You think he is still in Cape Town?"

"I do indeed, but that means your inside person at the bank may be in some danger."

"That is not good news. I will try to track him down and find out what he is up to."

"Be careful, Duncan. Remember what he did the last time in Germany to one of his own men."

"Will do. If you hear anything, please let me know. I do not want this girl on the inside of the bank to be in any kind of danger because of her help to me."

"Keep a lookout for him, and I will see what I can find out through our CIA contacts and our embassy security."

"Thanks, Alan. Let me know what you hear."

"Of course, Duncan. By the way, I checked in on Casey, and she is doing fine. She seems to be recovering from her gunshot wound very quickly. She is trying hard to be put on active duty again."

"I am sure she is very hard to keep down." Duncan hung up and headed back to the kitchen for a cup of coffee. The idea that Marlee might be in real danger because of him did not sit well. As he returned to the living room he heard the front door open. Marlee came into the room like a breath of fresh air.

"Hi, Duncan. Did you miss me?" She was smiling as she said this.

"Of course. How did your day go?"

"I've been very busy. We hired two new employees, and they had to have a training session this afternoon. That kept me busy. It's still better than me having to do the extra work they will take over going forward. But now, a glass of wine seems in order."

"Coming right up. Living room work?"

"Of course, tell me about your day."

Duncan told her what had transpired with Alan. She knew who Alan was now and understood. "How worried should I be?" She took a sip of the wine and looked at Duncan with concern.

"For the time being, I'm not concerned at all. We will have to be careful not to be seen together until we have tracked Assisi down."

"Since we are going to Stellenbosch and Paarl tomorrow, that should be easy."

STELLENBOSCH, PAARL

The drive was indeed uneventful. They had left at 6:30 a.m. and planned to meet Marlee's friends around nine in the morning at one of their vineyards. The drive was uneventful and really rather beautiful. The shanty town they passed along the way marred the view but was soon over.

"Who are we meeting, Marlee?"

"Two old childhood friends: Kip Van Sloot and his wife Yvonne. I have known them since the first grade in school. They own a small vineyard that makes a Pinot Grigio now. They are kind of trying to keep up with the trends. Most whites are easier to make than reds and do not require years of storage to be acceptable. They make a nice living with their vintage, which is generally accepted as a good table wine, although a blend."

"Sounds good. What do they know about me?"

"Not really much. I told them both you were working for the U.S. Federal Reserve as an investigator, but that is all. That is all I really know. Exactly what you do or how is foreign to me." There was no guile or guilt associated with her words. Still, again, Duncan realized how difficult the relationship was going to be going forward. There were times he had to do things that most people would find unacceptable if not immoral. It didn't matter if you were on the side of the angels or not. The realization came back again of how tenuous this relationship was going to be. With that thought, they pulled into the Van Sloot Winery. A wonderful setting with the mountains of Paarl as a backdrop. Both Van Sloots were standing at the front door of the main house as they pulled up.

"Welcome, both of you. I am Kip to my friends, and since Marlee is a friend, that includes you. This is my wife, Yvonne. Hi, Marlee, how are you?" He had a big smile on his face, as did Yvonne and Marlee.

"Hi, Kip, this is Duncan." They shook hands and were led into the house's living room. Yvonne busied herself with a coffee urn, and cups had already been laid out in preparation. They spent the next few hours on general questions of who was who, the past relationships and the status of the Winery. A fantastic Braivlees (S. African barbecue) was put on and enjoyed by all of them. It appeared as if Duncan passed muster for at least the time being. Duncan was careful to be circumspect about his job and current work, which was respected. They were used to Marlee being secretive about her work at the bank. He liked both of them. Yvonne said very little but observed everything that went on around her. She seemed protective of Marlee.

"We need to take a quick ride around the old winery. I promised Duncan I would show him where I grew up and the size of the winery."

"No problem, Marlee. When you are finished, come back here for a quick drink before you head home, OK?"

"Sure, thanks, Yvonne, and you too, Kip. It was a great day."

"See you both later. Enjoy the ride."

They took about an hour to visit the old winery, drive around the vines, and then head back to Van Sloots.

"They both seem very nice, Marlee. I understand why you keep them as friends."

"They liked you as well. You will see them again in the future. Right now, let's head back to their winery."

"Works for me. Your old winery looked very impressive."

"It is, and still produces grapes for KWV brandy. KWV has won many international awards for its brandy, and we were always proud of our contribution. I was sorry to have to sell it, but it was too much for me to handle. The Co-op that bought it is good people, and my parents would have been proud. They pay me a stipend each year as a part of the sale, and that is what allows me to live where and how I do." South Africa has changed over the years, but other than crime problems seems to be heading in the right direction. They continued their conversation on the Wineries in the area as they drove and then arrived at the Van Sloot's front door.

"Hi, Kip. I was impressed with the tour. We have a saying in the USA that the ideal woman is beautiful and owns a liquor store. I guess a winery is close enough."

"Well, Marlee is certainly beautiful, but I see your point. She does like the banking world, however, and through them, she has met you."

"I guess that side works for both of us. I do indeed like my end of the banking world."

"Well, you two, we have to get back to Cape Town, and it is already getting late. Hopefully, Yvonne will not be upset as we have to leave. We will be back. Next time we will bring more time"

"I certainly hope so. It has been a pleasure, Duncan. You are always welcome. Take good care of Marlee." With the final good-byes, Duncan began the drive back to the city.

"A very nice day Marlee. Thank you for introducing your friends. They were great and I will look forward to meeting them again."

They arrived back at the flat in the early evening. The sun had set behind Table Mountain, but light was still in the sky, although fading fast. Duncan unpacked the boot of the car and carried the wine case up to the flat. Kip had indeed been generous.

"Duncan, put a few of the bottles into the fridge and the rest in the hall closet. I know you will like these. I will look in the freezer and see what I can find us for dinner."

"After that barbecue, I am not sure I can eat a lot in any case." As he said this, his cell phone demanded attention.

"Hello."

"Hello, Duncan. New developments. Your pal Assisi has left South Africa and is on his way to Mexico via London and L.A."

"Where is he going in Mexico?"

"Right now, he is booked for Mexico City."

"Can we track him when he arrives?" Alan took his time to respond but then said, "Yes. I have called in some favors, and DEA has two operatives we can use down there, but time is limited. They will pick him up at the airport and see where he heads off to, but only for three days. I will book you out of Cape Town tomorrow morning, which can put you in Mexico City in two days via Rio. Tickets in your name at the South African Airways counter. You leave Cape Town at ten a.m. tomorrow." "Call me from Rio, and I will update you with whatever we have. Sorry to cut your vacation short, but this takes priority. You will be met at the Mexico City airport by two agents: Josh Halpern and Jose Fernandez, both DEA agents. Both are aware that you are acting under the President's orders."

"How did you accomplish that?"

"The President and I both agree that any large sum of money transferred to Mexico is not a good sign, so good luck, and keep me informed on what you find."

"Will do. Thanks for the arrangements. By the way, it has been some time since I was last in Mexico. Can you book me at the Zócalo Central Hotel, please? Make it for three days."

"Will do, and Josh will know that you are staying there. Once picked up, they will drive you to the hotel. They will meet you just outside of baggage claim."

"O.K. Alan, and thanks again. I will call you after I meet up with the two agents. I now have two more legs for this trip: first Rio/Miami and then Mexico City. Have a nice day; no sarcasm intended."

"I understand. It is a long trip. Stay safe and watch out for the two agents after customs."

"Will do. Anything new on Assisi?"

"So far, no. The Agents reported that they followed him to San Mateo Atenco, a large Villa near the Lake. Quite a beautiful spot, I am told. The Agents can fill you in on what they know."

"Where is this area?"

"It's not far from Mexico City. There is a lot of money in the area and very large homes in compounds. The security for the homes seems very advanced. There are lots of cameras, motion detectors, etc."

MEXICO CITY

The plane from Miami touched down in the late afternoon. Passengers disembarked without incident and headed toward immigration control. Duncan's one satchel bag hung from his shoulder. He always traveled light. Most of the passengers seemed like tourists, with a few businesspeople mixed in. The rush to immigration was like that of most airports. There was little point in rushing, as baggage claim for most would be arduous and slow. Duncan's passport was duly stamped with only a cursory glance at the bearer. He followed the small group through immigration doors to the baggage claim area.

The two DEA agents were waiting just outside of the baggage claim area as promised. Fernandez was easy to pick out of the two. He had light brown skin, heavy black hair, and the start of a beard. Unmistakable as a South American. Innes was guilty of stereotyping —certainly politically incorrect. Josh Halpern looked like any Ivy League graduate down to his penny loafers, blue blazer, and blonde hair. They would stand out as a pair in any crowd in Mexico. Not the best of disguises for DEA agents hunting drug lords. Inness approached the two of them as if he were an old friend, his hand extended for handshakes. Fernandez stepped forward.

"Mr. Innes?"

"Yes, indeed, Mr. Fernandez?"

"I guess we are rather obvious here," he grinned as he said this.

"I am good with the look if you are. The two of you together are almost invisible in the openness you present."

"Well, Mr. Innes, with your height and size, you are hardly inconspicuous. D.C. said you would be the largest passenger to get off the plane."

"At 6 feet, five inches, it is hard to hide, but it does discourage would-be muggers from taking a chance."

"I'll bet it does," said Halpern. "D.C. asked us to pick you up and take you to the Zocalo Hotel downtown. We can go over what they asked us to do, and what we have found out at the hotel. I would suggest we give you an hour in your room, and then meet again at the rooftop bar/restaurant. Great view of the central square and noisy enough for us not to be overheard."

"Works for me, and thanks for the hospitality. See you in an hour." They had arrived, and Innes went through check-in easily. His reservation was confirmed, and a room was assigned. The two agents proceeded through the lobby to the elevators heading to the rooftop. Duncan was escorted by a bellhop carrying his one bag to another bank of elevators and headed to his room. A quick shower to remove the travel patina would suffice, a few calls, and then off to the rooftop. The first call would be to Alan MacDonald, his boss in D.C. Alan's job as the new head of Security for the Federal Reserve made him a very powerful man. He had direct access to the President, if the need arose, and reported to the Chairman of the Federal Reserve. It was Alan who contracted with Duncan as an external investigator. Alan signed the checks for Duncan's work and travel expenses. If he wanted to be updated at any time, Duncan responded. They had become close friends over the years.

"I take it you are finally in Mexico City?"

"Yes, the two agents picked me up and I will meet with them here in about 30 minutes. The hotel is right in the center of the city on the Plaza Constitución. This spot should make it easy to get around. Anything new on your end?"

"Not to steal Fernandez and Halpern's thunder, I am told they followed Assisi to the El Guapo Hacienda."

"What the hell is an El Guapo?" Duncan was a little incredulous as he asked this.

"'El Guapo,' I am told means the handsome one.' This is a title also of one of the cartels down there. El Guapo himself is Luis Alessandro Garcia, the head of the Guapo Cartel."

"What do we know about them?"

"For starters, according to the FBI, the Cartel specializes in transporting illegal immigrants across our Southern borders, mostly in the Texas area. Some drugs, but small fry. They make a lot of money by transporting illegals. Some are women for the sex trade in the USA and others are just random refugees." They are well organized and, by all accounts, successful in getting a large percentage of their charges across the border." They have a network of transporters that pick the immigrants up and move them to their final destination cities. Costs to the immigrants can be as high as ten thousand dollars per person. Others are much cheaper at around one thousand dollars per person. The illegals are given false I.D. cards, driver's licenses, burner phones, and small backpacks with toiletries. The idea being that when dropped in another city, they look part of the scene."

"Well, what does El Guapo look like?"

"Certainly not the handsome one, as his name implies. He is about five feet seven inches and maybe 100 pounds overweight. The name shows a sense of humor, although his people would never laugh. There is an arroyo behind his hacienda that we believe is full of staff that did laugh. All of the cartels down there can be very brutal."

"How long have you two been doing these investigations?"

Halpern responded first. "I have been here for six years, and my partner may be four. My Spanish is not bad, but it helps to have a native speaker like José."

"Has all of this time been with the DEA?"

"Yes, since Trump, the DEA has been more active in Mexico. We were not aware of the Guapo Cartel until three years ago. A random arrest on the Texas border brought them to light. Now we suspect they move between 3,000 and 4 thousand people across the border daily."

"That is a logistical nightmare, or?" Innes directed the question to Fernandez.

"Yes, it is. It requires multiple safe houses for people storage on both sides of the border. Add to that the identity papers and other material, and you basically have an Amazon delivery system. Next-day delivery if possible. And you do not have to pay for PRIME."

"What nationalities do they transport?"

"What we have been able to track is mostly Colombians, Venezuelans, and Mexicans. Lately they have branched out to Chinese and Arabs. The Chinese are a bit of a surprise. Most of them seem to originate in Hong Kong or Macau. The Arabs are from all over. Lebanon, Syria, and Iran, from what we can tell. The Arabs have been contracting services from the Guapo Cartel in Kuwait. They pay cash up front, according to our sources in Kuwait City. They then fly to Mexico City, where they are met and transported to the North, which is very efficient and a real threat to us."

"How much of a threat?" asked Duncan.

"The ones we have been able to track head to the Northeast of the United States. They get lost in big cities like New York, Boston, and D.C. So far, we do not know what they get up to, but we're working on it together with the FBI. What is weird is that the ones we are tracking, in particular, are making contact with various student groups."

All three men ordered another round of drinks. The rooftop was filling up with visitors.

"Agent Fernandez, what else have you been able to find out? My real interest is Assisi, whom you followed from the airport."

"So far, very little. The first we have heard of Assisi is that you were coming to find out what you can, and we should offer any help we can. Care to tell me why you are interested, and in particular, how you have the clout to pull us off our current projects to chase after this Arab?"

"That part is simple. Assisi acts as a money man for a number of groups around the world, in some cases suspected terrorists. We became aware of him two years ago when he started transferring large sums of money to various organizations that we do not necessarily approve of their funding. The most recent payments went to Mexico, and we believe the Guapo Cartel was the recipient." I work for the Federal Reserve as an investigator and often look into bank transfers for the 'why's and wherefore's as it relates to the United States Treasury. My mandate is from the President and my boss is the head of security of the Federal Reserve. There in lies the clout."

"That explains why our boss in D.C. pulled us onto this task. But I'm not sure how we can help as we have no assets in the banking system here."

"You are helping already. I now know where specifically Assisi has headed. The next task will be, 'Why?' I would like to get a look at the villa El Guapo uses and where you followed Assisi."

"No problem," Halpern suggested. A road trip the next morning. Giving Duncan an evening of rest and sleep from the long flights was certainly welcome.

"Is this Villa far away?"

"No, a few hours should do it by car. It is in the town of San Mateo Atenco. The villa itself is off the lake on Calle S. de Mayo. A few good restaurants and great views in that area. How about we pick you up at 8:30 a.m. here at the hotel?"

"Great, that works for me, and thank you for your efforts to date."

"No problem, that's why we make the big bucks." Both laughed and called for the bill.

Duncan's room looked very inviting. A good night's sleep was a good idea. He would give Marlee a call in the morning to check in and then, after the visit to El Guapo's residence, give Alan an update. The two DEA agents had been friendly enough. Duncan liked Fernandez for his relative openness. Halpern was a little bit more taciturn, probably a result of years spent in a large bureaucracy. Both, however, seemed competent and fit. Fernandez obviously worked out, as did Halpern. Halpern was a little bit smaller and lithe, hiding an underlying strength hardly visible unless you knew where to look. Fernandez, however, looked like the type you would want as a backup in any dustup that occurred. What the two had missed at the Roof Top bar restaurant was a man at the bar paying close attention to the three of them. He had constantly looked over at Duncan and his companions as they drank their beers. What made him stand out to Duncan is the effort the man made to avoid anyone seeing he was interested. No eye contact, if at all possible. He seemed to know Halpern and Fernandez but not Duncan. Duncan's threat meter was ringing loudly as he passed the man on the way to his room. Innes made a point of mentally taking a picture of the observer for later reference. Once a threat was identified, it would stay on Duncan's radar until the mission was complete. This man was a fighter. Squared-off shoulders, small hips, large arms, and a bulging neckline. A scrapper without a doubt. Definitely a South American. As Duncan passed on the way to the lift, he could hear the man speaking Spanish into a now-open cell phone. Halpern and Fernandez reached the lifts at the same time as Duncan, seemingly unaware of whom they had just passed. Duncan glanced back to see if the man followed, which he did not. Once in the room, he quickly undressed, got into bed, and was asleep within twenty minutes. He called for a wake-up call at 6:30 a.m. That gave him enough time to shower and get some breakfast before he was to be picked up. His last thought was that he missed Marlee in Cape Town. More often than not, their nights together were short but effective. He always felt fresh in the morning and was pleased to see her asleep next to him. He would miss that here in Mexico City.

When the morning call came, it was a bit of a shock. He had slept soundly and really didn't want to leave his warm bed, but he would be picked up soon. First things first, he dialed Marlee's number.

"Good morning,"

"Good morning, Duncan. Have a good night's sleep? I didn't, as I missed you beside me. "

"I missed you too, but after two days on a plane, I slept like a rock. Now it's up and at 'em. Full day ahead. What about you?"

"Still training and handing off tasks to my new hires. They are coming along well, though. I did speak with Kip and Yvonne yesterday. They asked to be remembered. You made an impression."

"Hopefully, a positive one. I liked both of them as well."

"Positive indeed, but if you hurt me, expect Kip to come after you." She giggled as she said this.

"Understood, I will be careful. I have to go now, but I will call you again tomorrow. Have a great day, beautiful, and be careful." He hung up and headed down to the breakfast area. Breakfast was pretty much standard fare: an egg frittata, a scone, orange juice, and coffee. The coffee was more like a thick brown sludge but promised to be a good wake-up call. The spoon could stand up in the middle of the cup without support. He couldn't help but wonder what it would do in his gut. It held promise for a "rotor rooter" service in the future. Marlee's was much better and half as lethal.

Both agents came through the breakfast door at the same time.

"Is it 8 a.m. already, or are you two just early?"

"We are a few minutes early, but you're good. Finish up whatever it is that is resting on your plate, and we can go."

"What's on the plate doesn't worry me; it's the coffee that is a cause for concern. Do you want some?"

"No thanks, we have been drinking that stuff for two years and haven't died yet. What always surprises me is that whenever I return to the States for a meeting, the coffee is so weak I wonder why anyone bothers to brew it. If you are here for more than a few days, you will get used to it. Can't promise your gut will, but it is a great laxative."

"Okay, gentlemen, I get the message; I am ready."

Duncan took one more sip of the motor oil and stood, ready to leave. The room was empty of guests. All three headed to the door, with Fernandez leading the way. The agent's car was parked directly in front of the hotel. Fernandez was the driver, Innes took the shotgun position, and Halpern in the rear. Traffic was light, so it only took twenty minutes to get out of the city. Mexico City was built inside a giant caldera. The surrounding mountains are what held the famous smog in its boundaries. If you can't see the air, how do you know you are breathing? The air quality was reminiscent of Los Angeles. Children in both areas were unaware that the sun was yellow, not brown.

"How do you two breathe here?"

"Like the coffee, you get used to it. On really bad days, you cough a lot. On others, it's just part of the scenery," Halpern laughed.

"Does it make the backdrop a sorry yellow-brown?"

"Yes, Duncan, if everything is painted yellowish, you know you are in Mexico City. That's why so many people leave the city during the summer and head to the mountains and lakes. Air quality and cooler weather are the attractions. If you can afford it, you leave. If not, you hope no emphysema or asthma results from staying."

They passed through Toluca on the way to San Mateo Atenco.

THE VILLA

There were three obvious guards outside of the villa. They scanned each passing car. One of them had a cell phone, which he used to pass information on to the other end. The walls surrounding the Villa, looked unscalable, with barbed razor wire lining the tops. Heavy ivy did a good job of hiding the razor wire mitigating the look to a more acceptable facade. El Guapo took his security seriously. There were a number of CCTV cameras at each house corner effectively monitoring all possible entry points.

"Let's get into the center of the city and have something small to eat and a coffee."

Fernandez nodded in agreement while Halpern continued to check his rear via mirror as they drove.

"Sorry, guys, but it appears we have picked up a tail. A black Ford Bronco now about four cars to the rear. It came out of the Guapo Compound as we passed. Could be a coincidence, but I doubt it. It looked like he was waiting for us."

"Josh, have you seen the car before?"

" You are kidding Duncan or? The country is full of all terrain vehicles, large enough to transport at least 5 people."

"Well, pick a spot in town to stop, and let's see what the Bronco does."

"I saw a place on a corner as we drove in, about three blocks from here."

Duncan looked at Fernandez, who was busily trying to keep track of the Bronco behind them.

"Listen, Josh, just before we get there, stop at a corner so I can get out and take a look at the driver and any passengers. I will catch up on foot."

"This corner coming up should do the trick. A few trees block the view as you get out. Be careful; we do not know if we have been made. Now would be a good time to get out. Go about 1,100 yards from this corner to the restaurant on the right."

Duncan pulled open the door and quickly left the vehicle. As he did, the Bronco came into view as Josh and Fernandez pulled away. The driver was the same man who had been in the hotel bar the previous evening. He did not see Innes at the side of the road behind a tree. He was concentrating on the car he had been following. Duncan began to walk toward the restaurant keeping the Bronco in view ahead. Both the Bronco and Fernandez were slowing for a parking spot. There were a few pedestrians walking past shops and looking totally unaware of anything odd on the street. He could see Josh and Fernandez enter the restaurant. The Bronco drove past and parked about thirty yards from the entrance. Only one driver got out of the car, no passengers. He had a cell phone pinned to his ear and was talking into it keeping his eyes on the restaurant where Josh and Fernandez had entered. It was the same man from the rooftop restaurant bar of the previous evening. Just before the man entered the restaurant, he looked around to check the street. He did not see Duncan crossing behind him toward the same entrance that he was about to take. His eyes were fixed on the two Agents at a table next to the bar. The Agents were unaware of his entry and continued to scan the menu. He was pulling out a gun as Duncan entered behind him. Duncan saw the gun come out of the jacket and begin to swing towards the agents. He stepped forward and clocked the man on his head with the 45 he had carried on the ride. The South American went to ground as if he was pole axed, which of course he was.

Duncan stepped over the body and kicked the gun away toward Halpern who had finally stood up. Fernandez was talking to the other patrons and waitress trying to maintain calm. A few guests made it to the exit and kept going. Fernandez arrived at the body first as Duncan put his own gun away.

"Thanks for that, Duncan. It looks like you prevented one of us from buying the farm. How did you know?"

"This guy on the floor is the same man who was watching us last night at the Roof Top restaurant. I recognized him as he drove by following you two. Looks like your cover is blown."

What do you want to do with him?"

"Let's just leave him on the floor here and let the management team sweep him out with the garbage. We should, however, get out of here before the local cops arrive. Can't tell if he is connected locally, but probably. Most of the cartels own the towns they operate from. Come on, let's head back to Mexico City. Nothing more to do here."

All three headed toward the door. The waitress followed yelling at Fernandez as they reached their car.

"What did she want?"

"She wanted to know what to do with the guy on the floor."

"I told her to dump him in the trash around the back and gave her a few pesos to stop yelling. That seems to have worked for now, but let's get out of town."

Once back in the car, everyone breathed a sigh of relief. Josh was the first to speak.

"How did you know who he was?"

"I told you he was at the bar last night and paid too much attention to the three of us. When I saw him park, I just followed him into the restaurant. The gun came out of his jacket, so it seemed like a good idea to clock him on the spot."

"Agreed, and thanks, Duncan."

"Backup can work. I would assume that you would do the same for me?"

Both men nodded but looked sheepishly at Duncan. They decided to drive to Toluca, find a restaurant, and have lunch before going back to Mexico City. Toluca was much larger than San Mateo Atenco. The traffic was also heavier. Mexican drivers were similar to Italians. A four-lane road would suddenly become a two-lane road, with all of the cars racing to reach the two-lane before anyone else. Blaring horns, grimaces, and expletives were the order of the moment. Fernández remained unfazed.

"That restaurant on the left corner looks okay. What do you think?"

"Works for me; you are the driver."

"So far, no tail, so we should be clear to go. Let's park, have some coffee, and maybe an Arepa then off to Zocalo."

"Keep a lookout, everyone; let's not get surprised again."

They parked close to the restaurant. Innes scanned the neighborhood but saw nothing out of place. Halpern went into the café and looked around. He came back out and nodded, "All clear," to Fernandez and Innes. Once seated they all ordered coffee, some sparkling water, Arepas. The coffee still looked like motor oil but was loaded with caffeine. The water was warm but at least safe. No one wanted Montezuma's revenge at this point.

"Gentlemen, we have to pay closer attention going forward. I would not like to get jumped by Guapo's men again."

"Agreed, Duncan. We are all going to have to check in with our boss this morning or early afternoon. Maybe he has more information for us."

"Agreed, I have to call D.C. as well, but I can wait until later this afternoon. I am sure our friend we left on the floor will be coming back again. After all, he knows where we are in Zocalo. He didn't look like the kind that would let bygones be bygones."

"Probably not, Duncan. El Guapo has a reputation to uphold. Can't have his men be manhandled without repercussions."

"Where are you two staying in Mexico City?"

"We have an apartment not far from you. We will drop you off at the hotel when we get back and check in with you tomorrow morning."

"Okay, that works. We can compare notes on what D.C. has to say and what our next moves should be."

The drive back to Mexico City went without incident. As soon as they passed into the Caldera, the sun disappeared again, being replaced by a brown ball.

"This city has to be a dream for pulmonologists." "Doesn't matter; after a while, you get used to tasting the air. Occasionally, it even gets gritty." Halpern comment elicited a laugh from Fernandez.

"Not something I want to get used to, as I normally run at least 3 miles in the morning, and here that is not possible. I will be taking advantage of the hotel pool, but that is not enough."

"That is why our bosses envy our trips to the exotic areas of the world." Fernandez laughed again.

"You can keep 'exotic' if this is it," said Duncan.

"Well, maybe next time we will be sent to Bali, but I doubt it." Halpern seemed to enjoy the let's trash the area.

" I would not hold my breath," said Innes. "We always go to where the bad guys are. Although Bali has a drug problem, it's nothing like the cartels here."

"True, but we can always hope. And here is your hotel, Duncan. See you in the morning around 8 a.m.?"

"Works for me." He got out of the car, checked by habit the area for threats, and entered the lobby. There was a coffee shop on the lobby floor, which Duncan headed for. Although it offered only sludge, any liquid at this point was welcome. The waitress was comely but a little slow. Few people occupied the tables around the shop. Duncan sat at one and glanced around for anyone showing interest. The lobby appeared empty except for hotel staff. It had indeed been an interesting day. Now he had to explain to Alan Macdonald what had gone down. Nothing was really gained, other than that Compound Guapo was an almost impregnable fortress. It was time to get back to his room and make a few calls. Otto was worth calling as well in Germany. Maybe he had more.

"Alan, I'm glad you're still in the office."

"Sure, Duncan, but what do you have for me?"

"Not much. Went to El Guapo's Compound, drove around a bit, but they knew we were coming."

"How do you know?"

"They had a car waiting for us, which began almost immediately to follow us. I had to neutralize the driver in a public restaurant. The alternative would have been to let the driver kill the two DEA agents, which seemed like a poor idea."

"Agreed, but how did they make you?"

"I do not think they knew me. The Agents must have been made earlier, and they had us followed from Mexico City to El Guapo's." Duncan discussed seeing the man at the bar the previous evening and that he had been the same man as the driver Duncan had cold-cocked. "Too much for a coincidence."

"Be safe, Duncan. If they have made the two agents, you will be next. We now know that significant sums of money have been transferred by Guapo to agents of his in the USA. It appears that he has been financing some of the student unrest going on here. Over 2 million dollars found its way to Students for Palestine, which we can trace back to his accounts. Why Guapo would want to get involved in this is still a mystery." "The President wants you to look carefully into this and report back." If the Mexican Cartels are taking an interest in Middle East Politics in the United States, we want to know why. By the way, the two agents, Halpern and Fernandez are going to be given orders to track down the routes Guapo uses to get immigrants into this country. Feel free to tag along, but your primary mission is to find out the why."

"That might be problematic without gaining access to Guapo himself or his henchmen."

"Do what you can."

"I will call again tomorrow."

They hung up with Duncan, wondering how he was going to

handle this request. With the two agents compromised, the possibilities were very limited. He decided to call Otto.

"Hi, Duncan, you realize it is a bit later over here right now?"

"Understood, and sorry. Have you heard anything more about our Middle Eastern friends?"

"I did pick up a little gossip from Kuwait. One of our agents there overheard a conversation that he shouldn't have."

"It would appear that our friend Assisi may be making a deal to buy in as a partner in the El Guapo Cartel. Through such a partnership, they would be able to smuggle into the USA to handle their agendas, where and when needed."

"Seems a bit convoluted to me, but it does make some sense. Through said agents, they could transport money to finance some of their activities, and with expert advice from El Guapo, get quite a few people into the USA."

"Thanks, Otto. If you hear anything else, please let me know. Is this information from a good reliable source?"

"Yes, indeed. We make it profitable for our man there to keep us informed. We have been working with him for at least three years, and he has been spot-on, all the times he has reported. By the way, he hates Assisi. Assisi got him demoted over some petty issue two years ago."

"Everything always seems to reach back to Assisi. He is going to have to go one of these days."

"That may happen sooner rather than later as the BND has taken an interest in his activities. They do not play nice."

"Good to know. He is still here in Mexico, and I suspect, holed up in the El Guapo compound. I think I am going to take a few days and hang out near the compound. I would like to know when Assisi leaves and where he goes. Right now, I have two Federal Agents with me , but they may get very busy in the next few days, and that will free me up. Thanks for the update, Otto. I'll call you if I get anything of interest."

"Thanks, Duncan, and remember the BND might have people

there as well. You may be able to tap into them for some help. I'll check and let you know. Be careful."

"I will indeed. Call later today if anything pops up." Duncan hung up and immediately called Alan MacDonald in Washington.

"Sorry for the late call, but I just got off the phone with Otto Sternberg in Germany."

"Oh, what did he have to say?"

Duncan repeated the information he received from his call with Otto.

"If the Arabs are financing the Cartel here, that is bad news. I trust Otto, and that is what he believes. You will have to tell the President it looks like a new partnership between the Arabs and the El Guapo Cartel. If the Cartel specializes, as we believe, in getting people across the border into the United States and financing terror groups in the US, we have a problem. Maybe this will allow us to get ahead of these activities." "I suggest we use a new algorithm to look at transfers from Mexico and the Caribbean into the USA. While you are busy with that, I am going to camp out at the Guapo Compound and see if I can find out where Assisi is going next."

"Okay, Duncan. I will work on this from my end, but be careful. A lot of money is involved, which makes this doubly dangerous."

"OK, I will call again tomorrow evening."

Duncan took the elevator to the Roof Top for a late meal. Hopefully, the Guapo agent would not be there. He did not want another confrontation. That would happen soon enough.

Duncan arranged by phone for a rental car to be there in the morning. He was sure the two agents would be on the move after he had seen them in the early a.m.

RETURN TO THE VILLA

True to form, both agents arrived at the breakfast room a few minutes before 8 a.m.

"Good morning, gentlemen. Care for morning sludge and a roll?"

"No thanks, Duncan. We did speak with Washington and have an additional assignment beyond yours."

"Oh, and what might that be?"

"We're supposed to look into the routes of the smugglers of illegals into the U.S. We already know that if they start here in Mexico City, they will be transported through Saltillo to Nuevo Lareda or Reynosa and then cross into Texas. A few might go through Juárez and some to the New Mexico or California border."

"Okay, then now what becomes the course of action?"

"We are going to head up to Saltilloto and see if we can pick up a group heading north. We will follow them and see how they cross over, if possible. In the end, it probably doesn't matter. The USA side needs to start profiling people they run across, looking for Arab types. The hell with political correctness. As and when they stumble across Arabs and/or Iranians, they should be held for questioning. I would also like to know what they are bringing into the country."

"That seems a little like a hit or miss to me as a strategy." Duncan sounded very skeptical.

"Agreed, let's see if we can get lucky and spot some of them in Saltillo." They broke up at that point, with the two agents heading out to their car. Duncan's rental had just arrived. He signed the paperwork and gave the rental agent a credit card and a copy of his driver's license. He was free to head west.

The drive was quiet. He used the time to check his emails and tried to call Marlee in South Africa. No answer so she was at work and busy. He would try again that evening.

The Guapo Compound looked large before him as he turned onto its street. There were a number of cars loading up with quite a few people and bags. The Bronco was among them. It looked like five people per car and one or two children. He drove to the next corner and waited in an open parking spot. As the cars passed him by, he took pictures of the rear of each car and their plates, which he texted to Fernandez. These were the people they would follow when they reached the agent's stakeout spot. Finally, after a two-hour wait and multiple coffees, a limo pulled out of the Compound. The windows were all blacked out, only the driver was visible. The limo pulled to a spot two cars ahead of Duncan's and parked as well. The driver remained in the front while two doors opened in the rear. Out stepped Assisi and another person whom Duncan had never seen. They ducked directly into the Apothecary on the corner. Neither had seen Duncan nor even looked in his direction. As he was seated in the outdoor café, his height did not give him away. A few minutes after they had gone in, they both came out and got into the limo, which immediately pulled away. Duncan followed in his rental keeping an eye out for anyone following him.

They drove about thirty minutes and still had no tail. The road itself was quiet, with no other traffic. As they came closer to a gasoline station, Assisi's car indicated they were going to turn into it. Duncan continued onward, knowing, as he could see, there was no other way to leave the station, so they would have to follow. He pulled off to the side of the road about three hundred meters from the station, which allowed him to continue to observe the limo which was now being tanked up with gas. The stop only lasted a few minutes and then they pulled out onto the road heading in his direction. As they came close the limo slowed. The driver peered out the window at Duncan, as did Assisi who seemed to recognize him, said something to the passengers, and continued forward. Duncan started his rental and began to follow. They came to a crossroads of two dirt roads. The limo turned toward the right dirt road and the right rear window of the limo opened as they turned. A passenger leaned out as the turn was being completed. That gave him an unobstructed view of Innes's car. The first shot pinged the front of the rental. The second starred the passenger side of the rental's window. Duncan sped up heading toward the left side of the limo. Another shot seemed to bounce off the roof of his car. Dust from the dirt road was beginning to make the drive difficult.

Duncan decided on a "Pit" maneuver to stop the shooter and the limo from creating further damage. He eased his car closer to the left rear of the limo. As he came parallel to the limo and its left rear tire, Duncan swerved into the rear of the limo. The impact was immediate and loud. The crumpling sound of his rental boded insurance problems for the rental company. The limo driver immediately lost control of the vehicle, spun ninety degrees to the road, and then flipped onto its right side. This had the effect of an immediate stop. The shooter was now pinned below the right rear door of the limo. The driver had a nasty gash above his right eyebrow, which bled profusely. The passenger in the rear, Duncan could see, was Assisi as he had thought. Karma was a hard taskmaster. Assisi seemed dazed and partially out of it, but aware enough to grunt, "Hello, Mr. Innes. Duncan looked at the driver who now was leaning forward against his seatbelt, but in no position to stop Duncan from opening the rear door. He reached in took the brief-case that had been propped against Assisi right thigh. Assisi moaned and opened partially his eyes. One look toward Duncan, ignoring others in the limo. The shooter appeared dead and unmoving. Time to leave. Duncan returned to his rental, briefcase in hand, and started to drive back to the main road. He turned and headed back from where he had started. The trip to Mexico City would not be very long, but prudence urged that he get out of the area as quickly as possible. He passed through San Mateo Atenco without seeing another car or ambulance. The drive to Mexico City was quiet.

The rental he left in a parking garage near his hotel. He would have Alan Macdonald handle the return and any explanation required. His room had been cleaned up, with no sign of entry other than hotel staff. He threw the briefcase on his bed and started to make his phone calls. First on the agenda was Marlee in South Africa.

"I hope I did not wake you up."

"You did not, and I want to talk to you whenever you can. I miss you. Life is not the same since you left."

"Same problem here. Everything okay on your end?"

"Yes, Kip and Yvonne called, so I am going to their place for the weekend unless, of course, you're coming home?" She sounded a little breathless.

"Sorry, I wish I could, but not yet."

"Are you still in Mexico City?"

"I am, but not for too much longer. I suspect I will be going to Washington shortly and reporting back to work. I also wanted to ask you if you have a valid passport?"

"I do, but why?"

" I may be sending you a plane ticket when I know where I am going, and we can get back together. Do you have a valid visa for the United States in your passport?"

"I do. Two years ago, I had a conference in New York and was sent by my bank. Should still be valid."

"Great, let's see what happens over the next few days, and I will get back to you. Miss you."

"I miss you too."

The next call was to Alan MacDonald in Washington.

"Hi Alan, anything new on your end?"

"Not as yet, what about you Duncan?"

"There certainly is. I had a run-in with Assisi near the El Guapos compound. It ended well for us, but not so much for him."

"What happened?" Duncan asked as he described the events involving the two cars and the crash. He also mentioned the parking position of his rental and the fact that it needed to be picked up and handled.

"Have you looked in the briefcase as yet?"

"I have indeed. A number of recent transfers from Mexico to the United States. They were directed to various groups, including 'Students for Palestinians', 'Free Gaza' supporters, and a few I have never heard of as yet.

"Can you send me scans of these and anything else in the briefcase?"

"Will do, but mostly contacts in the U.S., which might be useful going forward. I think we should run them all down and also really go through his mini-Rolodex, which was also in the case. Right now, I think you and the President will be very busy with the contents. If Assisi is still working for the Iranians, this material is proof positive that they are behind the student protests at the U.S. Universities right now. Other than to embarrass us, what is the point? They are already winning the P.R. war against the Israelis unless they are planning something else and this is just the warm up. Assisi also recognized me at the crash site. "

"Duncan, did Assisi survive the crash?"

"As far as I know, yes. The shooter probably didn't make it, but the driver looked O.K., a little beaten up, but that is all. What I am sure of is Assisi will be very angry and looking for blood if he survives."

"Without a doubt. Let me speak with the President and see what he wants to do. I suspect you will be returning to D.C. in the next few days for a debrief. Call me tomorrow. How are the two D.E.A. agents?"

"I do not know. I had sent them the license plates and makes of the cars leaving Guapo's compound. They should have picked them up along the route they thought these cars would take. I will check in with them after we hang up."

"Stay safe, Duncan." The audible click ensured the call was completed. Another came immediately.

"Hi, Duncan. Thanks for the pictures. We were able to pick up two of the SUV's as they passed us in Saltilloto. We followed them to Nuevo Laredo. The drop-off point looked like a safe house adjacent to the border. We both think that they have a tunnel there over to the Laredo, Texas, side. The DEA and the Border Patrol have been alerted and will be waiting for the two groups on the USA side. Thanks for the intel. I will let you know if anything comes up from our end."

"Thanks to both of you. Let me fill you in on what went down over here." Duncan gave them the thumbnail sketch of the events leading up to the crash. He left out the briefcase information.

"Duncan, what are you going to do now?"

"I will probably be recalled to D.C. and see what my boss wants me to do. What about you two? More fun and games in Mexico City?"

"Probably. We will get marching orders in the next few days. Thanks again for the tip."

"My pleasure. Stay safe, as they say."

"We'll be back early evening tomorrow if you want to have dinner at the hotel Roof Top again. This time, our treat. I wouldn't want to overburden your expense account."

"Sounds good to me. I will be there starting at 6:30. Have a good trip back."

Duncan went back to riffling through Assisi's briefcase. He scanned all of the papers and contacts and sent them on to Washington. This would give Alan something to do. The cell phone in the bag really showed nothing, but the techies at home could have a look. Assisi was going to be highly irate. He left the TV, running in the background, but so far no news on the desert crash.

At 6 p.m., Innes took the lift up to the Roof Top to wait for Fernandez and Halpern. It had been a productive few days. If the two DEA agents had anything new, he would get it tonight. In the meantime, a glass of J&B with club soda would go down nicely. The bar was virtually empty, save for the bartender and a few waiters setting up for the dinner crowd. Duncan liked this hotel and the ambiance: quiet and understated. Not the usual blast of garish color so popular in Mexico. The sounds of traffic in the square below permeated the atmosphere and were acceptable at this time of day. As he ordered his second round, both Fernández and Halpern came into the bar.

"Gentlemen, I see you are none the worse for wear."

Both men smiled and looked around the area. No apparent threats, but with the day's activities, one could not be too careful.

"Hi, Duncan. It has been a long 2 days." Both ordered their own brand of poison with Fernandez ordering rum and coke, while Halpern had a gin and tonic.

"Did you find out anything more useful?"

"Not really, nothing in any case that we did not already know. The route was simple and quick for the SUV's. No one followed them other than ourselves. We made up a small convoy to the border.

"What about you? After the crash, any sign of the opposition?"

"Nothing as yet, but it is still early times."

"Yes indeed. Stay alert; El Guapo has a lot of agents in the area. You have embarrassed him, so he may feel the need for retribution. He does have a reputation to uphold. Now, let's get some dinner. Our boss won't pay for drinks but will cover dinner, so you can order anything you like."

"I'll put the drinks on my room. No worries, get a table."

Halpern jumped up and went off to the maître d'. Duncan and Fernandez followed.

"Thanks again, Duncan. If I get any information on the people we followed, I will let you know. For now, it was not a waste of time. We have a tunnel we were unsure of at this time. The Border Patrol will be pleased, as will our boss. Let's order and eat."

They sat at the table close to the edge of the balcony overlooking the square. Traffic noise still made it up to their position but was acceptable. A few more diners came in and were seated nearby. No immediate threats were apparent. They continued with small talk while constantly scanning any patron who came onto the balcony. Duncan was very interested to see if the man who originally had watched them turned up. Halpern and Fernandez both seemed a little jumpy.

"So, what is up with you two?"

Fernandez chose to respond.

"The group we followed was in two cars. A third peeled off and went elsewhere in Saltiloto. We are a little concerned about that car. We know the other two will be picked up by Homeland Security once they emerge from the tunnel somewhere in Laredo, Texas."

"OK, at least this is a good start. When will you hear about the first passengers you followed?"

"As soon as they are picked up by ICE, they will let us know. The question is, how many of these people are 'got-a-ways,' and who are they?"

"Agreed, but it is a start. Let me know if you hear anything from your side. I have been trying to get more information on El Guapo and Assisi through my channels."

"Certainly, Duncan, and thanks again for the license plates and car makes. Without that information, we would have missed this last shipment of illegal immigrants. They should be picked up on the Texas side shortly. I do not think they can keep them on ice too long."

"Let's hope so. I really want to try and understand the game plan."

Halpern responded, "We do as well. This operation of El Guapo is much bigger than we first thought.""I am sure I will be recalled to D.C. in the near future, but I would like to know a little more about the people who took the tunnel." "Agreed.. As soon as we have them, I will give you a call. We can go over theborder together,, and you can take part in the interviews if that works for you?"

"It certainly does, but you might find some resistance from border security."

"Maybe, but when they know you helped flag these people and the tunnel, they will be more likely to be cooperative."

"Great, I am going to get an early night and look forward to hearing from you tomorrow."

Duncan left the two agents sitting at their table and headed to the lifts and back to his room. It had been a long day; now it was just a waiting game. The bar was empty as he passed; even the bartender seemed to have taken the day off. There was enough time for a quick call to D.C. and although it was late in South Africa, he could check in with Marlee. He found himself thinking more and more about her each day. The time spent in Cape Town was a little dreamlike, almost too perfect. In his room, he checked his email, and there was one from Alan MacDonald with a request for a quick call. Duncan did as he was told and dialed Alan's cell phone.

"Hi, Alan, what's up?"

" I think you need to head home in the next few days. The President wants an update. He is still concerned about the Mexican connection. As a side note, I spoke with Casey, who is now fully recovered. She is back on duty. She is asking, 'Where are you? I gave her a thumbnail description of your recent travels. You may want to check in with her. She did, after all, take a bullet for you."

"Do not remind me. I still feel guilty about that one. I will give her a call and see her when I get back. Is there anything new on the transfers from here to the USA?"

"It would appear that El Guapo is now in the financing business of various student protest groups. We have traced three transfers via the SWIFT system to various student organizations. Two were direct to protest groups, which were used to finance the purchase of tents, camping equipment, flares, food, and outdoor clothes. We think the Columbia University protest was financed this way. The last transfer we are still trying to run down. I could use your help over here as soon as possible."

Duncan brought Alan up to date on the two DEA agents and the new tunnel found.

"I will be back by the weekend."

"Good, in the meantime, I will tell the President we can meet on Monday if he has the time. Considering the phone calls to date, he will have the time. Call me when your travel plans are firm."

"Will do. Right now, looking for a good night's sleep seems appropriate." They ended the call on that note, so Duncan dialed Marlee's flat. The chirping sound of her phone reminded him yet again of how far away she was.

"Hi Duncan"

"Hi, beautiful. How did you know it was me?"

"No one other than you would call at this ugly time. Still, I'm glad you did; I miss you."

"I miss you too."

They spoke for about half an hour after that. WhatsApp kept the price reasonable. If you had an internet connection, you could call virtually free.

"Duncan, I checked again on my passport, and it is good to go. Any idea when I can come?"

"Probably next week if you can get the time off. Plan on at least three weeks if you can get the time. I will arrange a ticket via South African Airways. They can get you to New York via London and then a short commuter to D.C., it's a bit arduous, but I can't wait to see you. I will pick you up at Washington National Airport. Let me know if you have any problems with the tickets. They will be business class all the way. I will leave the return open. Miss you and can't wait to see you again. I will call again tomorrow to see if you got the tickets and time off."

"Time off will not be a problem. I am owed at least six weeks from the past and the first few months of this year. Thanks, Duncan, talk tomorrow." When Duncan hung up, he emailed Alan and asked him to arrange the flights for Marlee. He knew this would not be a problem. Morning came too quickly. Duncan was excited to see Marlee again but also wanted to hear from the DEA agents. On cue, the room phone rang.

"Duncan here."

"We have our first break. The travelers were captured outside of the building where we thought the tunnel led. Two of the men were Iranians. We are going to head to the border in thirty minutes. Want to join us?"

"Absolutely. I should be checked out in fifteen. See you out front, and thanks for including me."

"No thank you is necessary; you saved our butts and gave us access to valuable intel to find the tunnel."

"OK, see you in a few." Duncan packed his bag and placed his laptop in the holder. Passport and other documents he might need, including his Federal Reserve I.D. case, he placed in his jacket pocket. Checking out seemed simple enough. The lobby was empty except for a couple checking out in front of him. The hotel had been what he expected, and he was satisfied. The checkout clerk gave him a copy of his credit card receipt and wished him a good day. Once outside, Duncan scanned the area for his usual threat assessment. Nothing out of the ordinary. Fernandez pulled up at the curb, and the doorman held open the passenger door for Duncan.

"Good morning, gentlemen. Road trip time." They left for the USA. Duncan kept checking for any tails, but nothing was visible. A little anticlimactic after the run-in with Assisi's limo.

"This drive is going to take about eleven hours to Laredo where we cross the border. We should get there about nine p.m., assuming everything remains quiet along the way. We will get lunch some-where along the way; otherwise, no stops other than a possible pit stop if Halpern's prostate requires it."

"Not fair, guys. My bladder is fine, it's my prostate that requires relief from time to time. Blame my genes if you must."

"I foresee a catheter in your future."

"Gee, thanks, Fernandez. Any other cheerful thoughts?"

"Not at this time. Just sing out with a little bit of warning when you want me to stop."

"Roger that."

LAREDO TEXAS, WASHINGTON D.C.

Duncan had called ahead and arranged two rooms for himself, Halpern, and Fernandez at the Staybridge Suites by the Laredo International Airport. The idea was that he could fly to D.C. out of this airport after they interviewed the two Iranians. Both Josh Halpern and José Fernandez were good with the idea.

"Okay, I have set up an interview with the Homeland Security people and the holding area they control in Laredo. Both prisoners will be available to us tomorrow morning after 8 a.m."

"Works for me. I have to check in with D.C. tonight when we arrive, but I'll be available tomorrow morning at 6;30 a.m. for breakfast. Will that work for both of you?"

"Sure, Duncan. And thanks for booking the rooms. There's the hotel, let's check in and see you in the morning."

They checked in and, tired from the drive, headed to their rooms. Duncan immediately called Alan in D.C. to report in that he was now on US soil.

"Sorry it's so late, Alan, but we just checked into the hotel in Laredo."

"Good, Duncan, see what you can get out of the two Iranians. The President is on for Monday morning at 10:30. I will pick you up at your condo at 10 a.m.. Call me if you get anything from these two clowns. By the way, Marlee will arrive on Tuesday afternoon at 5 p.m., from Newark at National."

"Great. Thanks, Alan."

"Will I get a chance to meet this lady? After all, she has given us a lot of valuable information."

"Sure, but let's give her a chance to get over jet lag."

"Fine, we can discuss it on Tuesday or Wednesday morning. Good luck tomorrow."

Fernandez and Halpern arrived, true to form, early. They got in the car and drove off to the detention center where the interviews would take place.

"Duncan, how do you want to handle this?"

"My first choice would be to waterboard them, but I am sure we cannot do that. As a second choice, how about sending the two of them to Fort Meade, putting them in protective custody, and handling the interrogations there? We have the capability of holding them for some time and possibly getting more information there than in this environment."

" We should be able to arrange that. If we run into any interference, can we get your people to put in a request?"

"Yes, indeed. I can handle that this morning, but we have to keep them away from lawyers or anyone else, for that matter. Let's see if anyone asks about them. In the meantime, let me send an email, and you will get a request quickly. What are the names they are using?"

"Our office here says they carried passports with the names Eddie Haddad and Mohammed Saleem, both aged 35 and born in Lebanon."

"Okay, I will pass that along. Let's start the interrogation and stall for a few hours to get the requests sent through and approved. I assume it should go through Homeland Security and the DEA?"

"Yes, we are going to have a report on that status anyway. Thanks, gentlemen, for the cooperation. If there is anything I can do for you, let me know."

They parked outside of the detention center and were escorted into the building by two uniformed guards with Homeland Security patches.

The prisoners were handcuffed to a table in a windowless room. Neither looked predisposed to speak with anyone.

"We want to speak with a lawyer," were the first words one of them uttered.

"Gentlemen, it will be a very long time before you can speak with an attorney. What do you think, Duncan?"

"I think it may be years before they see an attorney, maybe never." The two men squirmed in their seats, looking somewhat concerned.

"What we can offer you is a plane ride."

"To where?"

"You will see when we get there."

"You can't do this. We know our rights." The younger of the two was already whining.

'

"You have no rights; you are illegals caught sneaking across our border. You will be very lucky if we do not send you to northern Alaska and point out the direction of Russia, where you could swim to get away from us. A little cold up there, but we would give you a sweater. Of course, the question is, why are you here?"

Neither man answered. Both looked at the two agents and Duncan with some hatred in their eyes. A Homeland Security guard came through the door carrying a fingerprint kit.

"I have to get fingerprints on these two clowns."

"No problem, go right ahead." Duncan left the room and rechecked his email and phone messages. One email from Alan MacDonald said his request for Fort Meade had been handled and approved. They were to take the two pioneers to Lackland Air Force Base, where transport to D.C. was arranged. The two DEA agents were going to be instructed to go with Duncan and the two Middle Easterners. A van would arrive shortly at their current location and pick them up for the drive to the San Antonio area. Duncan came back into the interview room. The use of the Laredo airport was no longer a possibility. San Antonio was not that far away and would do for a quick way to the D.C. area. He appraised the two DEA agents of the plan as he understood it. Now they would just have to wait for the van. Four hours later, they were all strapped into a government Cessna Citation on their way to Washington and Fort Meade, Maryland.

"Well, Duncan, if you have to travel, this is the way to go." A uniformed Air Force female brought them all coffee. The two prisoners were given a glass of water each. The flight was uneventful, if not boring. Neither prisoner offered up anything of value. They still called for a lawyer every 15 minutes or so. The penny has as yet not dropped and was never going to happen. The captain came on the intercom with a landing warning in thirty minutes. The stewardess cleaned up the cups and water glasses. The descent was marked by a lower pitch of the engines and the sinking feeling as ground effect began to make itself felt. The plane landed at Andrews Air Force Base. There was plenty of security and no witnesses to who got off or on the Citation. They taxied to a Navy hangar where a black limo was waiting with an obvious guard at its side. Fifteen minutes after landing, they were all bundled off into the stretch limo. Duncan sat in the front with the driver. The two prisoners and DEA agents sat in the rear. The agents handcuffed the prisoners to the door handles and made themselves comfortable for the ride to Fort Meade.

"Driver, how long to Fort Meade?"

"It's only about 35 miles, sir. In this traffic, maybe thirty-plus minutes if there are no major traffic jams."

"Great, I am tired of just sitting around." Duncan took out his cell phone and called Alan MacDonald. The boss liked to know where he was whenever he was in the D.C. area. The call was short indeed: drop the prisoners off at the equivalent of a brig. They drove along Route 32 and turned onto Route 175 toward Fort Meade. Duncan noticed the parked truck on the side of the highway in front of the U-Haul facility. It looked out of place considering the parking lot was just off the road. As they drew parallel with the truck, an RPG was fired at their limo. There was nothing the driver could do as the weapon obliterated the front end of the limo, putting what was left into the ditch. Duncan bailed out and put himself between the smoldering limo and the parked truck. The driver remained seated and bleeding in the front seat, which had been partially destroyed. The prisoners were still in the car and remained handcuffed in place. The agents had also bailed out and had taken up positions near the truck but were protected by the ditch.

"You two, okay?"

"We are good. Poor shot considering how close the truck was. A few feet farther back and we would all be dead. Did you see anyone?"

"No, I think it was set off remotely."

The sirens could be heard nearing in the distance.

"Take a look at our guests. How are they doing?"

"Both alive and breathing. Haddad is going to have a monumental headache, but otherwise unscathed."

Two M.P. Jeeps arrived along with the local constabulary. All had blue lights flashing and were followed by a fire truck and an ambulance.

Duncan yelled out to the MPs, "Secure the area and the U-Haul center." This put both M.P.s in motion, now with guns drawn, running toward the U-Haul building. The other jeep stopped by Duncan and asked for IDs. The agents produced their cred packs, as did Duncan. They explained that they had two prisoners in the back of the limo. The prisoners were removed and handcuffed to the jeep.

Duncan walked over to Haddad, who appeared slightly dazed. Saleem was none the worse for wear. As Halpern drew closer, Duncan saw he was bleeding from his right shoulder. A large piece of glass poked out of his jacket. This was the source of the blood. The EMT was beckoned over to take a look. The jacket was removed, the blood flow staunched, and the shoulder bandaged.

Two more cars arrived, with a lieutenant colonel coming over to the four of them.

"You certainly know how to make an entrance. I assume one of you is Innes?"

"Yes, sir, that would be me."

"Got it, let's head back to the Fort and put your prisoners where they cannot do any harm." They all trundled off to the two cars: Duncan with the colonel and the others in the second car. Halpern stayed with Duncan and the colonel.

"Mind if I make a quick call, Colonel?"

"Go right ahead; we will be on the base in five minutes."

Duncan dialed Alan, and they discussed what had happened.

"My question is, how did they know to hit us by Fort Meade?"

"I do not know, but someone leaked the information. Maybe at Laredo if you were overheard making travel plans? Otherwise, no one on this end knew the plan. Is everyone all right?"

"One of the agents, Halpern, was slightly injured by flying glass; otherwise, all was well."

"Duncan, the President has assigned a top interrogation crew to go after the two Iranians. By the time they are finished with them, we will know everything there is to know. I suggest you leave them and get to your flat. I will call you tonight. Stay safe. Your colonel there knows to supply transport to your home. Both DEA agents will be picked up by their H.Q. staff. Talk later." Alan hung up.

Duncan waited for the other DEA agent to arrive, and they exchanged phone numbers that would work in the Washington area. That done, Duncan and the colonel headed for the military sedan and returned to the city.

"Quite some excitement, Mr. Innes. Who are these two you brought as prisoners?"

"Possible terrorists."

"They apparently do not trust our people with the job."

"It's not that Colonel. There is a very real threat and we need to understand the extent of it before things get out of hand. In short, the pressure is on to squeeze these two for what they know. I would strongly urge you to stay as far away from this as possible. Keep your staff separate as well, and leave the team to do their thing. The less you and your people know the better. Security has to be an issue. You saw how far the opposition is willing to go to eliminate these two men. Firing RPG's near Fort Meade takes Chutzpah as the Israeli's are want to say."

"This event will certainly cause us to step up security both in and around the base."

"Good, the main thing is we keep these prisoners alive and your people safe."

"Agreed. Our security teams are already reevaluating our protocols and assigning new troops to the perimeter. Your prisoners are safe now. The two agents will also be picked up today. The man named Halpern seems to have a serious shoulder injury from the glass fragment. He should be okay in a few days." "The one named Haddad has a severe headache already." "He will be in a lot of pain tomorrow." "The medics will take care of him." "If you must come back to Fort Meade, please leave your friends with RPGs somewhere else. One day you will have to explain how you have so much juice to be able to get the entire Fort to handle your two prisoners."

"I'll try, but I can't guarantee that it will be possible. Suffice it to say, you are better equipped for the task at hand than any other facility in the city. Thanks for the ride, Colonel; I appreciate it."

"My pleasure, but I would prefer that if you visit again, you please leave the RPGs behind."

"I will if I can, Colonel, and again, thanks for everything. Try to keep the base scuttlebutt to a minimum." Duncan got out of the military vehicle and entered his condo building. Everything looked quiet. There was some mail at the front desk that had been held for him, as his box was now full. He retrieved the overflow and headed up to his flat. His cleaning lady had recently been there. He could always tell when she was in his flat. The place looked spotless: no glasses in the sink, curtains drawn, bed made, suggesting a very meticulous person was the resident. A magazine he had been looking at when he left was still on the coffee table, but now it was folded closed and neatly placed on a corner of the table. The first order of business was to give Casey a call. He tried her home, but no joy. Maybe she was working again, so he tried her cell phone.

"Hi, Duncan, are you home now?"

"I am. How are you doing? Back at work, I believe?"

"Yes, no residual problems, just a larger promotion. But next time, please do not get me shot to get the promotion."

"Sorry, Casey, but thanks for saving me. Lt. Fisher must be happy that his case is solved."

"He is indeed, although he is still a little bit annoyed that you were so unavailable. I believe Alan MacDonald took care of that through his channels."

"I am sure he did. Do you want to catch up for lunch tomorrow?"

"Sure, how about 1 p.m. at la Perla. I know you love that place, and I am in George Town in the morning, so that works for me."

"See you then. Do you always work on Saturdays?"

"No, on a rotation, but this weekend I am on duty."

"Okay, until then, I look forward to it. I'll try to ensure that you are not shot again."

"Gee, thanks. Have a good evening."

The pile of mail was mostly junk: flyers for every type of appliance known to man and a few new restaurants in the area promising superb culinary delights. It did not look appealing. There were just so many ways to fry chicken, and hamburgers no longer held appeal. He was glad to hear that Casey was doing well and did look forward to seeing her again. Alan had done a good job of keeping him out from under the police microscope, which the president probably assisted with, as usual. Casey's promotion was certainly deserved. He listened to his answering machine on the landline phone, but there was nothing of interest. Tomorrow, he would take care of any outstanding bills that needed his attention and get a good workout in the gym and a long run. It was time to get back into a real routine. Exercise was a habit, and if lost, it had serious consequences. Monday morning was the meeting with the president, and

Tuesday, Marlee would arrive. He was shocked at how much he looked forward to seeing her again and holding her in his arms. He also knew she would be exhausted from the long flights from Cape Town to Washington. As he was thinking this, the cell phone went off.

"Hi, Duncan, care to get a drink at the Whale?"

"Sure when?"

Alan MacDonald suggested in a half an hour.

"See you there." It was a short walk over to Whale. They often met there. It was never too crowded, and although happy hour was now, it would gradually slow down to about one hour. A quick shower and a change of clothes, and he would be ready. As Duncan left his flat, he did the usual check scan for new threats, of which there were none. His street was quiet, and it was a short walk to the Whale. The bar had the obligatory twenty or so hangers-on, and a few of the tables were taken. None of the people he could see looked interesting. As he scanned, Alan MacDonald entered and headed over to him at the bar.

"I'll have what he's having." Another scotch and soda was placed before him, and Duncan nodded his approval.

"It certainly has been exciting being home. A little less excitement seems called for at this point."

"Agreed, but Duncan, you do have a way of attracting unwarranted attention."

"I know. Did you hear if they caught anyone in the Fort Meade area?"

"So far, no one has been found. The Van was stolen this morning and reported properly. The RPG was fired from the front of the Van. The FBI has taken over the case for two reasons: one being the event occurred more or less on government property and two, local police do not have the forensics capability. Hopefully, they will turn something up. Our two friends, Haddad and Saleem, are proving difficult, but the interrogation team believes they will break them by tomorrow. We will see. Right now, I want you to stay safe."

'
"Sounds like a good idea to me. How is Halpern doing with his shoulder injury?"

"As far as I know, he will be fine. He lost some blood but is doing well considering. Both Fernandez and he are being debriefed on their entire mission now by Homeland Security. The President will have the updates for us on Monday morning. What do you think about Fernandez and Halpern?"

"Both are competent agents. They certainly know their way around Mexico. I suspect that Fernandez is a little annoyed by the attack. He seems the type to carry a grudge. Halpern will shrug it off but will want to jump back into the fray."

"Well, that's good. Both of them are being reassigned to full-time El Guapo monitoring. The discovery of the tunnel system has made this cartel a major point of interest. Add the Iranians to the mix, and you see the issue. The DEA has seconded them both to Homeland Security for the time being. I think they will be going back to Mexico in the coming week."

'
"Now, what about you? How are you holding up? RPGs and car crashes make for a busy lad."

"I am fine, although I am looking forward to Marlee coming on Tuesday."

"How about I get to meet her on Wednesday evening? I'll make a reservation at the Capitol Grill, which I hope she will enjoy."

"Sounds good, but let's not overwhelm her with too much detail on what is going on over here. Agreed?"

"Certainly, just a friendly dinner. Do you think she might enjoy meeting the president?"

"I am sure she would, but let's keep it low-key, please."

"We can discuss this on Monday morning with the president."

"Fine, let me bring you up to date with what transpired in Mexico and Assisi."

What followed was a blow-by-blow description of the events leading up to the attack at Fort Meade.

As Duncan put all of this into words, he again realized how lucky he had been. For the most part, Alan just listened. He realized as well how close a call Duncan had endured. It was a brazen enemy indeed that was prepared to fire RPGs on American soil near a military base. He might have lost Duncan to this one.

"We have taken care of the car you wrecked down there. It will come out of somebody's budget, but for now, it is no longer important."

"Thank Alan. It would have been awkward trying to explain the damages, in particular, the bullet holes. I suspect it might be difficult for me to get another rental if I am down there."

"That is probably true, Duncan, but there is really no need for you to go back right now. The President has alerted the FBI to our Mr. Assisi, who will be tracked if he leaves Mexico. Any information gathered will be forwarded to my office, but Mr. Assisi is now on a very short leash. The FBI is also trying to identify all of his colleagues, including the gentleman you gave such a headache to near El Guapo's compound. Take it easy tonight, and I will pick you up Monday morning at 8 a.m. "Get a good night's rest and take Sunday off. I'm sure the President will have a number of questions." Duncan got up and headed to the door. The whale was quieter now. Once outside, he saw Alan's car waiting, gave a nod, and went home. The street was virtually empty. No threats were visible. He found himself looking forward to Marlee's arrival. He made a mental note to fill up his fridge and get some flowers for her arrival. Saturday noon, Duncan entered the main door of la Perla. A fair number of tables were already full. With the hospital nearby, many of the patrons were doctors or nurses. Casey was seated near the front door with her back to a wall. She waved to Duncan as soon as he entered.

"You are looking none the worse for wear. I heard about Fort Meade and just knew you were involved."

" I had two prisoners from the Mexican border in tow. They were dropped off at Fort Meade for debriefing, and I came home. You look well, how is the shoulder?"

"Well, my pro aspirations on the tennis circuit have been cut short, but otherwise, I am good. A little stiff in the morning."

"I wanted to thank you again for saving my bacon that day on the Circle. By killing Matsumoto, you reduced Lt. Fisher's caseload. He must be pleased?"

"Still a little miffed that you were not around for further interviews, but the call from the President put that to rest. Alan was a charmer, and it certainly helped having the President turn up at the hospital. I became an instant celebrity. I am sure that was part of my promotion, but let's not do that again. Alan said you went back to Cape Town to a lady friend there?"

"Yes, I had met Marlee on my last stint in Cape Town, and we became very close. She was a big part of our success down there."

"Well, I almost don't believe that someone has finally captured the elusive Duncan Innes."

"I guess if it wasn't going to be you, someone had to do it. I can't keep running into beautiful women and not have some feelings arise."

"I am happy for you, Duncan. Try not to get her shot if possible. Does she know what you do for a living?"

"More or less. She is less than happy with my travel schedule but is accepting."

"Well, that makes her unique. If I recall, Jessica, your lawyer friend couldn't handle that from the get-go."

"You are probably correct."

"So this is serious on your part?"

"Yes, it is. The biggest problem is that she lives halfway around the world."

"I hope it works out for you, Duncan. Perhaps a good woman can domesticate you to a degree. I do not envy her the task."

"Thanks, Casey. We shall see. Right now, she is flying to Washington from Cape Town and will be here on Tuesday."

"I would love to meet her. We can exchange war stories about Duncan Innes."

"I am not sure that is a good idea, but if possible, I will arrange it. You were and still are a big part of my life, as is Marlee."

"I will look forward to it, and do not worry, I will not embarrass you. Maybe just a little to watch you squirm." Casey smiled as she said it. Duncan knew both women would like each other. If he was prepared to have Alan MacDonald meet her, why not Casey?

They spent another hour discussing his mishaps in South Africa and then Mexico. He couldn't tell her everything that had happened but gave a good thumbnail sketch.

"Stay safe, Duncan."

"You won't do anyone any good dead!" Duncan nodded in agreement.

"Sorry to cut this short, but I have a lot of shopping to do. Monday will be busy, so I need to stock up today. The fridge is bare, and I need some flowers, etc., to spruce up the place."

"My God, Duncan, you are becoming domesticated. I must meet this Marlee."

"You will soon enough. By the way, good luck with the new job. Stay safe, and if you need anything I can supply, just call."

"Will do, and have fun shopping."

The rest of the day was spent shopping for groceries and flowers. It required two trips, as he did not realize he owned no flower pots or vases. A sad state of affairs. Once home with the new vase and groceries, he settled down for a relaxing afternoon. No emails, no phone calls; a quiet day indeed.

The President

Alan Macdonald's limo was outside Duncan's apartment building, as promised at 8:00 a.m.

"Here is a cup of coffee for you, Duncan. Ready for the president?"

"Yes, sir. Not sure that I can add much to what he already knows, but perhaps he has some information for us."

They drove to the White House, following the same procedures as last time. This time, however, they were led to the Oval Office, not a meeting room. An orderly took their coffee orders and pointed to the sofa in the middle of the room. The President walked in through a side door and approached the two men.

"A pleasure, Alan, as always, and you as well, Duncan. You two have been busy."

"Yes, sir. Can you bring me up to speed on the Fort Meade event?"

"Nothing much to tell, other than what I am sure you know. We both believe that the Guapo Cartel was behind the attempted hit. I think, and Alan agrees, that the two Iranians were not supposed to be captured and certainly not interrogated."

"That is what the interrogation team suggests as well. You seem, Duncan, to have a knack for stepping into difficult situations. I am thinking, of course, of the lovely Casey that Alan had me visit in the hospital. I assume she is fully recovered now?"

"Yes sir. She also got a nice promotion, so is very happy. Thank you for visiting her in the hospital; I know she appreciated it very much.

"As you may know, Alan and I were roommates in college at Purdue; he doesn't ask for much, but when he does, I try to comply."

The President opened the file folder he had brought with him into the room.

"Gentlemen, the interrogation team has filed their initial report. They have been very quick, but I understand they used an enhanced interrogation protocol and some chemical enhancements. Normally, I would not be happy with their use, but in this case, it was justified. They also believe there is much more to be squeezed out of these men, but it will take weeks to months to have them completely debriefed. The early findings are Saleem is just a gopher for Haddad. Saleem was supposed to keep Haddad safe on the journey. He obviously failed."

"Do we understand why they are here, sir?"

The President looked at his open file again.

"Haddad is a facilitator for the Iranian Propaganda arm. His task is to foment unrest within the U.S. in any way he can. Right now, he is essentially funding Student unrest on behalf of Hamas. He has a network of operatives throughout the country. This network has taken the last five years to build. Many of their people are exchange students. Others are within the Iranian and other diplomatic core cadres. The feeling is with constant agitation from the students, they will be able to build on Americans' disgust with the entire Israeli issue and basically politically force us out of the support of Israel. Iran wants to have a greater say in what goes on in the oil-producing states. They would seem to believe if Israel falls, the last buffer between Iran and Saudi Arabia is gone. They believe that there is enough anti-semitism in the US to bring this about. Iran as a free agent, without any constraints in the region, would be a disaster. Follow that up with their shortly being a nuclear power and you have a recipe for war. We cannot have Iran controlling all oil and energy from this region. That would cripple our export markets in both Europe and Asia. The result would be Iranians having a permanent gun to our heads. We cannot let Israel fall. Geographically and strategically they're extremely important. Israel can control access to the Suez Canal. If Iran does build their proposed pipeline through Iraq, Syria and Lebanon, Saudi Arabia becomes a minor abstraction. Keeping us constantly putting out fires here is a good strategy for them. It has the side benefit of making Iran, in the eyes of the Arab world, a major source of power and support. They will have brought the great Satan to their knees. All of the northern Arab States, such as Syria, Lebanon, Iraq, Jordan, and finally, Egypt and the Mediterranean States, will fall into line. With the Islamic population growing exponentially in Europe our traditional allies will be lost. Kissinger, in the sixties, had warned that the next great threat to Europe would be Islam. He was and is very right. There are parts of: France, Germany, and the United Kingdom today that are predominantly Islamic. That population is overwhelming the local cultures in many countries. The implications are vast. Something similar is going on in the USA, with the Latinos overwhelming traditional white Anglo-Saxon culture. In another fifty years, more people will be of Latin derivations than Europeans. Already now, many Americans are speaking Spanish as their mother tongue, with English being the second language spoken at home. Turn on your T.V. and see how many ads are now spoken in Spanish. The stronger culture will win. With the population growth of Spanish speakers and illegal immigration, we are losing the battle to keep America for Americans as we know them. The great Protestant work ethic may or will disappear. Can't help comparing all of this to the great migrations across Europe thousands of years ago. Our challenge will be how well we control and foster assimilation. Rome suffered the same challenges."

"What are your advisors saying at the NSA?"

"The general view is that Iran wants to reestablish the Persian

Empire like Cyrus the Great once did thousands of years ago. Keep in mind that the Persian Empire extended from Iran throughout the Middle East to India and present-day Turkey. Add Egypt, and you have an Empire like the Ottomans, only bigger. The only bulwark hindering them is the Israeli's. Currently, they hope for disgust from the American population and abandonment of Israel. Their 5th column of elected officials in our country add to their overall goals. By fomenting protests, riots, and terror attacks, they succeed in undermining American influence in the world and specifically in the Middle East. There is no need for armies; just overwhelm the local culture. Look at the rapid expansion of Islamists in Europe. In another fifty years or so, the Islamists will represent a large proportion of the European population. They will never have to fire a shot and win. States like Michigan and Minnesota are going Muslim. The current world 'Cyrus the 1st' is winning. Our culture will fail, we will lose our friends

"Duncan, they agree with me on support for Israel. The question is how do we respond to all of this? Do we allow these demonstrations? Do we start a P.R. campaign against it?"

"Right now, what I would like, is for you to follow up on Haddads' mandate and see where the threads take us. Look for cells of Iran on our soil. Allan, what are your suggestions?"

"I agree with you. I believe that Duncan should go down this rabbit hole and see where it takes us. I also think it would be helpful for him and I, to have your direct sanction to pursue this, regardless of where it takes us."

"That's fine Alan, however, I want to be kept informed on what you are chasing and how it goes. I will have my secretary give you an official written order in this regard, and some phone numbers should you run into any interference."

"Thank you, sir, I suggest that the NSA and the FBI be told Duncan here is acting on your behalf."

"Will do Allan. In the meantime, if we get anything more from Haddad, I will let you know. "

"Thank you, sir. As I report directly to Alan, he can keep you up to date on what findings I uncover. The young lady from South Africa that has already helped us uncover so much is arriving tomorrow afternoon. As she and I are very close, she will be staying with me. If there is anything new, I will let you know."

"Do you think she would like to meet me? You both could come to the Oval Office again and I can thank her for what she gave us last year."

"Yes sir, I am sure she would love to meet you. How does Thursday look for you?"

"Thursday morning works for me. Can you get here around 11 a.m.?"

"Yes sir. I and Marlee Johansen will be here."

"Great, I shall look forward to meeting her. For now, you two have to leave as I have a meeting with some congressmen in a few minutes. Thank you for stopping by and Duncan for all you do for our country."

They left the White House and headed back to Alan's office building. They did a post-mortem in the car.

"That went well Duncan, now we have to deliver. With Marlee here will that slow you down a bit?"

"A little bit, but I'm sure I can work my way around it." They arrived at Alan's office, parked and went up to his floor. The first order of business would be to get all of the wire transfers from El Guapo and his accounts to where ever they were sent. That should give us a starting point. Alan nodded his head in agreement and promised the information for the morning.

"I want to check in with Halpern and Fernandez and see how they are doing."

"Go right ahead, but I doubt they will be able to give you a lot. Halpern is recovering from the glass shard in his shoulder and Fernandez is waiting for his reassignment."

"How do you know Alan?"

'I checked in with the head of the DEA this morning before picking you up. He said Fernandez was being sent back to Mexico. Halpern will follow in a week or so. Their task down there is incomplete. The DEA and NSA want more information on the El Guapo Cartel. Since both Halpern and Fernandez have experience with this Cartel, they are the obvious choice to follow up."

"Ok, I will give Fernandez a call and see if I can help at all. Hopefully, they'll keep us informed on what they discover going forward. I am sure that EL Guapo is now at the center of the protest activities in our country."

"Good idea, at least it is a starting point. I will have the security office scan all of the transfers from known Guapo accounts and try and put a road map together for you. "

"Thanks Alan. I will talk to you later today if Fernandez has anything new. Otherwise, is dinner still on for Wednesday evening?"

"By all means. You, Marlee and myself. Let's say at 7 pm at the Capitol Grill."

'We will be there. Have a great day and stay out of trouble. Your staff can start to put the transfers together for me."

"Talk later. I want to follow up on whether Assisi is on the move or not. The NSA is tracking his movements. Once I know I will call you. Say hello to the lovely Casey if you see her. She is impressive in her own right."

"I certainly will, and again Alan, thanks for getting the President to visit her in the hospital. This was very much appreciated."

The two separated as Duncan made his way down to the lobby and an Uber to get home. Meeting the President and getting a written mandate to pursue Assisi's endeavors would make life a little easier. He checked his cell phone messages and found that Marlee had written she was on her way. Tomorrow at Washington National would make for a great day. He was very much alive with anticipation. They had only been apart for a short time, but for Duncan it was too long. The ride back to his condo was short and thankfully uneventful. Still, some last minute chores to do prior to Marlee's arrival. He took the elevator up to his floor. No one around, everything looked quiet. His cell phone began to ring as he entered the Condo.

"Hello."

" Hi Duncan, Josh Halpern here."

"Hi Josh, how is the shoulder?"

"The Medics got all of the glass out, but still sore. Probably stay that way for another week or so. Should have a great scar. Will make a great bar story in the future."

"Can you tell me now, just what I got myself into through you?"

"Not really, Josh. As I told you before we are interested in an Arab who seems to be behind many of the student protests in this country. He was staying with El Guapo. You and Fernandez had followed him from Mexico City Airport to Guapo's Compound. Our question was why did he go to Guapo's H.Q..?"

"Well, this Assisi seems to have a pretty long reach. It is not everyone who can organize and fire an RPG at a government limo in front of an Army Base. So far our people at DEA and other assets of Homeland Security have not been able to find the would-be assassin. The Base Commander is very upset. Security has been bolstered with our two assets being questioned there, it is almost impossible to move around the base. Fernandez has been shipped back to Mexico and I will join him next week. What are you up to now that Mexico is behind us or at least you?"

"For the next week or two, not much. I have a visitor to take care of and then I will be back to work. I had wanted to speak to Fernandez, but if he is in Mexico, I will leave it for the moment."

"Try and stay safe. They tried once to get us; although we may not have been the targets, they may try again."

"I will certainly try. My H.O.A. would not like RPG's going off in the building or environs. You stay safe as well in Mexico. When you reconnect with Fernandez give him my regards. If you two come up with anything of interest, please give me a call. I may be able to help. I certainly want to stay up to speed on what El Guapo is up to for now. Have a good trip back to Mexico and stay safe. El Guapo might not be too friendly having you two looking into his activities."

" I am sure he would not be happy. We will see. Thanks,

Duncan for your help to date. I will get back to you if we find anything out about Assisi. Stay safe yourself."

Duncan hung up and returned to the kitchen to continue preparations for Marlees' visit. His Condo was not ideally equipped for such a good cook as Marlee. He ensured that there were a few bottles of wine in the fridge and enough: eggs, bread and cold cuts for sandwiches and fish in the freezer for at least one dinner. A few steaks in the freezer rounded out the meals for the time being. Vegetables in the fresh produce slot. They would be going out for most meals. But better prepared than sorry. He answered his mail, both written and email type. Anticipation of tomorrow was now making itself felt. No new news from the President's office or Alan. The old saw of no 'News is good News', sprang to mind. Assisi kept coming up in his thoughts. What was he up to and how would that affect the USA? The President was concerned and Alan shared that concern. If Assisi, and through him, Iran, was really behind the student Hamas protests, would that be the extent of it, or was something else being planned? Not enough information as yet. The attack at Fort Meade suggested something much larger afoot. The attention span of America was short-lived at best. If the protests continued, the public would tire of it and they would fade away from the public consciousness. That certainly was not positive for Israel, but half the country did not understand why America was so supportive of Israel in the first place. Most did not understand the strategic importance of a foothold in the Middle East. The world still revolves around energy. U.S. export markets needed to be able to purchase American goods and agriculture. To do that, they needed viable economies. The loss of energy would crash their economies and because of this, our export and economy would also crash. Israel was our ace up a sleeve should an evil player such as Iran decide to bring down the West. By fate or accident thereof, Israel was central to Middle East stability. Israel would become our jumping-off spot, if needed, to restore order in the oil-producing countries. Secondarily, Israel's intellectual property capacity was huge and largely benefited our economy. Medical research, A.I. research etc., and defense knowledge all ultimately benefitted the U.S., which made it imperative we support their efforts. It was a small price to pay considering all of the pluses we gleaned from Israeli activities. Watching television news was depressing. The chants of from the river to the sea were idiotic. No one seemed interested in protesting the British or French for their complicity in the Middle East debacle. After all, without the Sykes Picot agreement of 1916, the Balfour declaration of 1917, Israel would never have come into existence. Israel owed their very existence to the hubris of the two major Colonial powers of the time. Palestine for Palestinians was absurd. Palestine never existed as a country. The Sumerians and Akkadians etc. along with other tribes never enjoyed a country called Palestine. History should be taught in schools rather than the histrionics of today. Israel was a positive force for the region, if and when the locals understood the benefits they could reap from Israel's existence. The truth was no one in the region wanted to house the Palestinians. They had tried to overthrow the Jordanian king and Egypt's government in the past. Wherever they went, they were met with skepticism and distrust. In short for all of the neighbors of Gaza, no one wanted them in their country. History had taught Jordan, Saudi Arabia and Egypt well. The feeling was leave them to Gaza, let them self-govern and they would implode by themselves. Many of the other Arab countries believed that they should remain an Israeli problem. Just stay out of our countries. Self-determination in a country the size of a large city in the USA would ensure they failed. They would never be able to build a sustainable country called Palestine. Even if they expanded tourism for beaches, hotels and ancillary amenities, they would fail. The work ethic was lacking. Duncan decided on that note to get a good night's sleep and be prepared for Marlee's arrival tomorrow. The phone remained thankfully quiet.

The morning came early. Duncan decided to go for a run and then workout to clear out the cobwebs of a good night's sleep. The streets were quiet. It was only 6:30 am. The overachievers were already out and about. Office buildings in the area had lights burning on most floors. Few pedestrians were moving allowing Duncan a straight shot to the park. Once around would do it and then to the gym. He kept a locker there with a fresh set of clothes to walk home in rather than the sweaty shorts and tee he used to run in the early am. An hour on the various machines available finished off his morning routine. A quick shower thereafter and he was ready for the day. As usual, he checked the area for threats when he reached the street level, to head back to the condo. No one of interest was apparent. A short message on his phone said Marlee was in Newark and would be at National on time. He felt the rush of excitement at seeing her again in a few hours.

Marlee Johansen

He took an Uber from his Condo to Washington National Airport. Traffic was the usual afternoon rush. The airport, while convenient to the city, sat between multiple highways going in and out of the Washington D.C. area. The Pentagon proximity did not help the congestion. It often seemed as if everyone wanted to leave at the same time. He couldn't get to the gate to greet Marlee, but could stand at the baggage claim area and watch the bags travel in their never-ending circle. Her carousel was labeled Newark, and bags began to arrive, as did a few passengers. Everyone seemed in a rush to get bags that would take their own sweet time arriving. A crowd began to form around her carousel. He saw her coming off the escalator that led passengers to their bags. He felt his heart begin to pound at the sight of her. She waved before he could get to her. Both moved a little faster in their approach as she traversed the open area.

"My gosh, you are a sight for sore eyes. I have missed you."

Marlee smiled.

"Me too. It's been a long flight but it was worth it when I saw you. Right now, how about a kiss and hug."

"Absolutely. Welcome to America and Washington. Hopefully, the flights were not too bad? "

"Not at all. Flying First Class helps a lot. I do not know how people at the back of the bus survive those flights."

"Well, let's get your bags and get back to my condo. I am afraid it will not be as grand as yours."

"No problem, as long as you are there with me. "

Duncan took her hand and headed over to the baggage carousel. Marlee pointed out her bags, which he retrieved. They walked to the exit door and Duncan called for an Uber.

'Uber is cheaper here than owning a car; no parking problems, no insurance or gas expense."

"We have Uber as well. And I agree, unless you have to go great distances, it is hard to beat."

The car arrived a few minutes later and Duncan found himself behaving like a teenager. He couldn't stop looking at Marlee and smiling. She reciprocated. He held her hand tightly the entire trip back to his Condo.

"How was the flight or flights better said?"

"Long, but okay. I slept a lot of the way. Newark was a nuisance having to change terminals and the long walks. But then again after sitting in airplanes for so long, the walks felt good. I was surprised by the number of fast food spots and donut shops abounded. No wonder this country has a weight problem. I felt I could gain weight just walking past Cinnabon. The bars were also full of what looked like business people imbibing whatever was available. A noticeable shortage of children, but that was probably a good thing. Quiet flight from Newark to here. Of course, seeing you on arrival made it all worthwhile."

"I couldn't wait to see you. I do have some surprises for you. You are going to meet my boss Alan MacDonald tomorrow evening over dinner, and the President would like to meet you on Thursday for coffee if you are up to it? Also, my old friend Casey, whom I have told you about, would also like to meet you. I am a little concerned about that meeting. "

"I would love to meet her, but why Alan and the President?"

"Alan and President Evans are both college roommates and each want to thank you for your help in the early Assisi transfers. The information helped plug a major leak to terrorists in this country. Besides which, I did tell them how beautiful you are, so curiosity prevails. I hope that is O.K. with you?"

"Absolutely, and in particular Casey since she is an old girlfriend of yours, perhaps I might gain a few tips and warnings?"

" That is what I am afraid of when you two meet. I am sure you will like each other or I wouldn't have agreed to a meeting."

"Not to worry. If you like her, I know I will as well."

"We have arrived. This is my flat or Condo. There is no great view unless you like brick."

"This room is lovely Duncan. The flowers look great. Where do I put my bags?"

" The master bedroom is straight ahead. The closet on the left is now empty in preparation for you. Plenty of hangars. Towels in the bathroom through that door. Now I need to hug you. I can't believe you are here."

They embraced for what seemed like hours, with intermittent breaks to put clothes away and continue to unpack. If they had been a few years younger, the giggling would have been a distraction. But both were so happy to be together again that it was ignored.

"How about a glass of wine. Sauvignon blanc? I like Kim Crawford from New Zealand if that works for you. No South African wines are available here. It's a little on the sweet side, but tasty."

"Sure Duncan, but since I have you here with me, the wine is just a small plus. I am not too tired to take you to bed right now. So hurry up and get a glass, I do not want to wait."

Duncan immediately did as he was told with enthusiasm and speed!

The morning brought sunshine into the Condo. Duncan got up and went to the kitchen to start coffee. He pulled out three eggs and started to make an omelet for their breakfast. Three slices of toast, butter on the table, and two coffee mugs. He had purchased some melon as well and placed the slices in the middle of the table next to the butter. As he put the plates down next to the burner,

Marlee came into the kitchen wearing a robe and nothing else, or so it seemed.

"Good morning sleepy head. How did you sleep?"

"Once you let me go to sleep, Duncan, it was fine. You certainly proved last night that you missed me."

"I was very happy to see you again, and again and again."

"Down Tiger. I need some recovery time and breakfast. "

She reached around him giving him a kiss and hug that was obviously heartfelt. Yet again he felt his pulse skip a beat.

"Please keep that robe closed or we have to go back to the bedroom."

Marlee laughed but complied.

"It is nice having you to myself again Duncan. I have missed this." Her smile lit up the room.

"The eggs are done. One slice of toast or two?"

"One slice is fine."

She pulled up a chair at the table and started to sip her coffee.

"So what's on the agenda for today?"

"A little sightseeing. I will take you to the normal tourist spots this morning. We will probably go to the Mall and the World War II Memorial. Then off to the Lincoln Memorial, followed by Chinatown for lunch at Jackey. We should be back here around three in the afternoon. Take a shower and get ready for dinner, and then off to meet Alan MacDonald, my boss, at a nice steak house, which I am sure you will enjoy.

"You do not have to play tour guide Duncan. I am happy to be here with you."

"As am I, but you never know when you will be back, so let me show you around a bit. For now, since breakfast is finished, let me clean up and shower and we can be off and do the tourist thing."

"I like having a man make breakfast and then surprise, surprise, actually clean up afterward. "Give me a half an hour and I will be ready."

"No worries, that works. This kitchen will only take 15 minutes than a shower. Half an hour works."

One hour later, both were off to the Mall and a walk to the World War II Memorial.

"Duncan, this is certainly a beautiful Memorial. The walk past the Viet Nam memorial was also quite impressive. "

"I'm glad you enjoyed it. I lost a lot of friends in Viet Nam and also in Iraq and Afghanistan. I often wonder if it was worth it or did we just satisfy the egos of politicians?"

"Probably the latter. No war is ever really won. The winner erects statues, the losers bury friends. What is left behind are often times a disillusioned population. If you drive around London or Pretoria, you will find Memorials to the fallen and heroes. I wonder what solace their families take from these monuments. Wouldn't they have rather wanted to have their loved ones home, not buried on some battlefield no one can pronounce?"

"I agree, but there is a thing called duty to country. If you love your country you will do anything to protect it. It doesn't matter that the leaders are corrupt or misguided. I saw a lot of kids get killed. They all were prepared to die for their country. Being let down by leaders is just part of the game, sad though it may be."

"Well, on that note, it's a bit depressing; let's go get some lunch."

"A walk through Chinatown will be fun and there is a restaurant there called Jackey Cafe. I am sure you will like it. Just stay away from anything labeled Hunan or Szechuan. They are extremely hot and there is not enough water in Washington to get you past the burning in your throat."

"What do you like Duncan?"

"I like their shrimp with walnuts or their fried noodles. Their duck is also good if crispy. Or I can order both and we share them?"

"Now that sounds very good. "

"Both meals are very light as is most Chinese food. Tonight will be a bit heavier at the Steak House. In this country people say you can eat Chinese, but you will be hungry again in about two hours."

"We say that as well. Probably universal throughout the world. I shall look forward to it."

Marlee leaned over in the Uber and gave Duncan a kiss on the cheek. She also pressed his hand to her thigh as they drove through the city to Chinatown. The car pulled over to the curb in front of the café. Large arches of Chinese design spanned the street. Many of the shops displayed knockoff art and sculptures for the tourists. The smells were powerful. Peanut oil was distinctive as was the spices and pepper smell emanating near the sidewalk. If you stayed in one spot too long, your eyes would begin to water.

"Ok, let's get some lunch and then head back to the Condo to get ready for tonight."

Preparation for dinner included an afternoon tryst in the bedroom. They couldn't keep their hands off one another. Two showers removed any remnants of the afternoon 'delight'.

"You are indeed energetic Duncan." She was smiling as she said this.

"You were not exactly an unwilling participant. Shall we get ready for dinner?"

"Of course, it wouldn't do to keep your boss waiting. How formal do we have to dress for this dinner?"

" I am wearing slacks and a blue blazer. You could come in sackcloth and ashes. It wouldn't matter, you will be the prettiest woman in the place."

"Thank you, kind sir, but I did bring a cocktail dress so I shall be fine. I could however use an iron to get the travel out of the dress if available."

"No problem, in the hall closet you will find an ironing board, virtually unused, and an iron."

"I would offer to help, but I am sure a burned dress would not be a good idea."

One hour later, they were dressed and off with an Uber to the Capital Grill. It was a short trip. The bar area looked empty as they entered. The reservation was found and they were seated as Alan came through the front entrance.

"Good evening Folks."

"Good evening Alan. May I introduce Marlee Johansen to you Marlee this is Alan MacDonald."

"What a pleasure Ms. Johansen. I have heard a great deal about you from Duncan. Although he did tell me you were very beautiful, the understatement is quite evident."

Marlee blushed and smiled, lighting up the room.

Duncan responded with "Down boy, she is taken."

"Please call me Marlee, Mr. MacDonald"

"Thank you Marlee and I am just Alan."

"Just Alan is like saying Atilla the Hun was a wayward tourist."

"Well, it's your party Alan, so please have a seat."

"My pleasure Duncan. Have you had a nice day in Washington?"

"Oh yes. Duncan showed me around the Mall, the Lincoln Memorial, and the Viet Nam and World War II Memorials. Chinatown for lunch and then home to get ready for tonight. "

"You have been busy. Make sure Duncan takes you out into the countryside as well. I know you are having coffee with the President tomorrow morning which he insisted on. Your help in the past is much appreciated and the President wanted to express that appreciation in person as do I tonight. You may have saved many lives with the help you gave Duncan last year, and we appreciate that very much."

"You are welcome, I was glad to help, although I am sure I broke many rules in giving you the transfer data. It was for what seemed like a good cause at the time."

"It certainly was, I think we should order now. Would you care for a drink?"

"I would indeed, perhaps a California red wine since we are in a Steak House."

"Yes, how about a Rutherford Hill Cabernet Sauvignon? You do not see them very often in restaurants, but one of my favorites."

"Sounds good to me."

"Duncan, that work for you?"

"Yes, Alan. Your party, your choice. I have been drinking more wine in the past year since meeting Marlee than in the last fifteen. It is a good habit."

"My, My, Marlee. You are a good influence on our Duncan. Please enjoy the wine, and here is a toast to you and your stay in America. I hope you enjoy it."

"Thank you, Alan, I am sure I will."

At that moment, Marlee gasped and waved to another woman that just came into the restaurant. The newcomer waved back and came over to their Table.

"Always a pleasure to see you, Marlee. How is Cape Town?"

"Very well Madam Ambassador. I have not seen you in the bank for some time, but I guess you are over here now representing us to the Americans."

"I am indeed, but always pleased to see a fellow South African."

Both men stood up as soon as the woman arrived. Marlee made the introductions. She explained how she knew the Ambassador, Mrs. Nomainda Mfekato through the bank.

"Would you care to join us Madam Ambassador? "

"Thank you Mr. MacDonald but as you can see, the two gentlemen fidgeting at the bar are with me. They are both South Africans from home who are also long-time friends. But, thank you for the invitation, and Marlee, as always a pleasure. Please enjoy your holiday, and no offense to Mr. MacDonald, but I see Mr. Innes is worth visiting, assuming of course that is the case?"

"It most certainly is Cathleen. I hope I may still call you that when we are not working?"

"Certainly. Enjoy your dinner, and it was a pleasure running into you here, goodnight, gentlemen."

As the Ambassador left, the food arrived.

"A happy coincidence Marlee. I hope you enjoy dinner."

"I am sure I will but honestly, as long as Duncan is with me I know I will enjoy everything."

Alan looked directly at Duncan and said, "You lucky dog."

"Don't I know it. Now let's enjoy dinner. Cheers!"

The dinner went on for another two hours as no one was in a rush.

The bill was paid by Alan and thank you all around.

"I will see you both again tomorrow at the White House. Have a good night."

"Thank you, Alan, I am sure we will." She squeezed Duncan's hand as she said this.

All three departed at the same time. Marlee gave a small wave to the Ambassador as they left.

The wave was returned and then she shook hands with Alan thanking him again for the lovely dinner. The ride back to the condo reminded Duncan how important Marlee had become to his life. She leaned against him in the car and smiled as she reminisced over her time in South Africa with the Ambassador. The smell of her hair was enough to trigger thoughts of how wonderful she really was. The condo was a little anticlimactic after the excellent dinner. They both were happy to be home again.

Marlee went to the restroom while Duncan prepared to go to bed. Tomorrow would be an early day. The President at 11 would require some preparation. Marlee emerged from the restroom in her robe. Her hair had been pulled up and pinned in place. A rush of warmth passed through Duncan as he watched her come over to the bed. He was reminded yet again of how wonderful she was and how she completed his life. He threw back the covers to invite her in with which she complied. Her hand went to his chest she laid her head down on his shoulder. The smell of gardenias filled the room. He reached over and pulled her closer. A small giggle escaped from Marlee's and he kissed her. Rising passion ensured sleep would take some time to come. Neither seemed to mind. She kissed him again, noting his excitement.

The morning brought sleepy eyes to the forefront.

"That was a night to remember Marlee."

"Indeed it was, many more to come I hope?"

"Certainly, although perhaps better in Cape Town. Still I have to work. Today's visit to the President will be pleasant, but I suspect he will be pulling me off to the side to increase my workload. Do not be upset. Alan will keep you company if that happens."

"I understand. I am Jealous of your time, but I do understand." She was smiling as she said this. The room lit up with that smile.

"We have to get ready. Alan will pick us up at 10:15 to ride over to the White House. The meeting will be informal. There is quite a process we have to go through to get into the White House. I hope you do not mind."

"I am sure it will be fine. I need about an hour to get ready, so let's eat breakfast and I can start."

"I was planning on taking you back to bed young lady. You are just too delicious to let wander about in the Condo without supervision."

"Thank you, but first impressions are important. Eat breakfast first then get ready. Tonight is another thing in any case. Do not look so forlorn Duncan."

"Yes, ma'am. Eggs, toast, coffee and O.J. coming up."

One and a half hours later and they were ready for Alan's car to arrive. Once in the limo, both men began talking about the Fort Meade question in an abstract way. Neither seemed prepared to bring Marlee into the conversation. They pulled up to the White House and started through the same process as in previous times. The only difference was the extreme attention the guards afforded Marlee and her smile.

"I really should bring you here more often. The process was so much more pleasant with a beautiful woman as a companion."

"Duncan behave! This is my first time meeting the President of the United States. Quite some occasion to enjoy."

They were ushered into the Oval Office. The same orderly offered coffee or Tea. Undoubtedly in respect for Marlee and the South African beverage of choice for the morning. As the coffee was served President Evans entered the room.

"Good morning everyone. Duncan, Alan and this must be Ms. Johansen?"

"Yes sir, an honor to meet you."

"If all my visitors were as pretty as you, I would make it a habit every day to have you drop by. Unfortunately, the Speaker of the House does not meet your standard. But welcome, I do appreciate you taking your vacation time to visit. I hope that our friend Duncan here, is making your stay pleasurable and rememberable."

"He certainly is sir." Again her smile lit the room charming both the President and Alan.

"Good, then let me first thank you for helping Duncan with the information you supplied in South Africa. As I assume you are aware, not everyone is interested in helping us in these tumultuous times. Your giving us copies of those transfers, was most helpful. I cannot thank you enough."

"Although I did have some ethical concerns while doing it sir, I am glad I did. Terrorism is everyone's concern."

"Agreed but accept a thank you from a grateful nation. I hear you ran into Ambassador Mfekato last night at the Capital Grill."

"We did indeed, she is an old friend and it is always a pleasure seeing her. How did you know so quickly?"

" I would love to say I know everything that goes on in D.C. but that is not the case. One of the gentlemen at the bar noticed your exchange with the Ambassador and reported it back through channels. Nothing sinister in that, but my staff is very protective."

"I understand sir."

"Good, well if you do not mind, I would like to take Duncan away from you for just a few minutes on another matter. Alan can enjoy your company for a while if you do not mind?"

"Of course not. Just please do not take him for too long."

"Just a few minutes, Duncan would you please join me in my other study for a few minutes."

They both got up and left the room. It was hard for Duncan to leave Marlee behind. They both sat in a study-like room adjacent to the Oval Office.

"Duncan we are getting more information from Haddad at Fort Meade. Your guess that El Guapo was somehow deeply involved with the Iranians is valid. There is now a partnership between Iran and the El Guapo Cartel to ferry operatives and cash in and out of Mexico. These first two, Haddad and Saleem are just the beginning. They have a type of underground railroad, which is planned to be expanded over the coming years. Using the Guapo Cartel to get money and operatives into the USA represents a real and present danger. The DEA has seconded their agents to the NSA to gather further Intel in Mexico. Now, how do we best use their presence there? Can you tell me a little about the two DEA agents you worked with in Mexico?"

Duncan went into a description of both men, their competence and dedication to the job. They were in deed the right people to take the lead on the El Guapo Cartel.

"I would like you and Alan to keep tabs on both agents. It may mean you have to go back there, however, I am concerned that this cabal between Iran and the Cartel may prove very dangerous. If the Cartel continues to fund the student movements and it spreads, there is no telling where it will lead to. The NSA is also concerned and is putting pressure on everyone involved for more information. We have the Democratic convention coming up and the Republican one shortly thereafter. Both are likely targets considering the number of people that will attend. With that in mind, please contact the agents and see what they are up to, and if you need any support or run into interference, use the numbers I gave you. Short of the 6th fleet, anything you need is available."

"Thank you sir. Anything new from the two prisoners?"

"So far nothing more than what you already know. If I get anything, I will pass it along through Alan or by phone. Please keep me up to date on your progress."

"Yes sir, I will."

"Good, on that note, let's return to Alan and your lady friend. I must admit I am jealous. She is a keeper."

"That she is sir." They returned to the Oval Office.

Alan and Marlee said their good-byes, and all three headed out of the office, escorted by a secret service gentleman. Their limo reappeared, and Alan suggested he drop them both off at Duncan's Condo.

"Thanks for the ride back Alan."

"Don't mention it. Marlee you were the hit." They both laughed. Small talk ensued all the way back to Duncan's Condo.

"Anything you want to tell me, Duncan?"

'Nothing new. As we both suspected, the President is concerned about the Mexico connection and wants me to continue looking into this, which I will do. Right now, however, I would prefer to concentrate all of my attention on Marlee. She is only here for another two weeks."

"Understandable, and I do not disagree. Hopefully, she will have a good time and get some sightseeing in while here."

"Gentlemen, remember, I am still here in the car with you."

"Sorry, Marlee. Since Duncan was taken away by the President, I naturally want to know what went on in the other office. "

"Yes sir, I understand. But now that we are back at the Condo, would you like to stop in and have another cup of coffee?"

"No thank you Marlee. I have plenty of work to do at my office and need to get back. I hope you enjoy the time here and as we often say, have a nice day."

"Thank you, Alan." They both left the limo and headed into Duncan's Condo building. Once in the condo itself, Duncan's cell phone began to chirp.

"Hello, Casey, how are you?"

"I am fine, how about you and Marlee? We never did plan a time to meet again. Any suggestions?"

" Sure how about La Perla tomorrow night at 7 pm?"

"Works for me, what about Marlee?"

"She johwns I was going to set this up, so I am sure she will be fine with it. Will you make the reservation or should I?"

"I'll take care of it. See you tomorrow evening. Bye"

"What will I be fine with now?" asked Marlee.

"That was Casey, and we agreed to meet her tomorrow for dinner. I assume you do not mind?"

"Not at all. I am looking forward to it. I really would like to meet her and compare notes."

"That is what I am afraid of at this point. I am sure you will like her, very down to earth, and really quite striking."

"Don't worry, I doubt she will create a problem for you and I certainly will not. What should we do for the rest of the day?"

" I thought I would take you walking along the Potomac River. Parts are really quite pretty. Since we have been sitting so much a little exercise will do us both good."

"Good plan, when we get back, I will cook dinner Duncan. I saw you have some fish in the fridge, so I have something to start with and can go from there."

"OK, that settled, let's go for a walk."

The walk turned into a three-hour trek. It was kind of fun for him to see her take in his home area and enjoy their mutual company. The weather remained kind, which was not always the case in D.C. They passed a few other walkers along the river bank. He continually scanned for threats, but was pleased there were none. As they turned to head back, his cell phone chirped again.

"Hello, Duncan here."

"Hi Duncan. I have just been on the phone with the BND in Berlin. It would seem that our Mr. Assisi has been very busy in the USA. I believe he is on the way to Washington as we speak. Be careful. He will recognize you."

"Will do; thanks for the warning, Otto. Any idea what he is up to?"

"Yes, he is continuing to support anti-Israeli groups on behalf of Iran and Hamas. The men assigned to El Guapo's compound in Mexico reported there was a lot of activity at the Compound. Mostly Americans that dropped by. We are trying to identify them now. If and when I get anything more, I will let you know."

"Thanks Otto, I trust you know of the attack on my limo at Fort Meade. We have two of Assisi's men in custody. Someone tried to silence them and me in the bargain. So far all we know from them is that Assisi is financing a number of anti-Israeli student groups at Columbia and California."

"To what end Duncan?"

"Beats me. It is just another distraction, but there is propaganda value in each protest. Looks good in the Arab world. Kind of like a magician gets you to look at one hand, while all the action takes place in another. A few of the politicians play along adding credence to the complaints of the student groups. It is amazing how quickly everyone forgets October 7th and the massacre. That Hamas could have stopped the destruction on day two by just surrendering is ignored. They have killed their own people. Now, everyone pretends to be outraged. We have the attention span of gnats and certainly no memory of how this all started. Our leaders are just as corrupt as Hamas and some of the Israeli's. Are the BND men staying in Mexico now?"

"Yes, but not much going on, other than the Americans passing through Guapo's compound. With Assisi gone, they may be reassigned shortly."

"How many are there watching the Compound?"

"I am told three are three of them. Why do you ask?"

I may ask you for a favor shortly while they are still on site."

"Ok, let me know if anything comes up."

"Will do Otto, and thanks for the heads up. In the meanwhile, any chance of getting intel on the number of people in the compound?"

"I can only ask Duncan. If they know, I will let you know."

'Thanks, Otto, as usual, I owe you one."

They chatted for a few more minutes and then hung up to go about their business. Duncan immediately sent off a text that Assisi was on the move, and it looked like Washington was his next stop, per Otto Sternberg. Once back in the condo, Duncan poured two glasses of wine. Once again, they sat in the living room and enjoyed each other's company. A habit he could easily get into in the future.

"Duncan, I need about 45 minutes for our dinner to be ready.

Does that work for you with all of the phone calls you are getting now?"

"That works, thanks. Here have a glass before you start to cook."

The look he gave her brought a smile and a tinge of redness to her cheeks. She also could get used to this proximity very quickly. As she took a sip, her cell phone chirped.

"My turn Duncan. Just a minute."

"Go ahead, I'll wait."

"Marlee here."

"Yes, sir, I am in D.C. at the moment; what can I do for you?"

"Yes, sir, I will call you back, probably tomorrow, with the schedule."

"Duncan, that was chairman Devilliers in Cape Town. He needs me to go to a banking conference in London next week. Would I be able to cut my holiday short and handle that? Of course, I will have to go. That means our time together will be cut short. I would leave next Wednesday evening to arrive in London the following Thursday. The conference starts on Friday morning and goes into the following week. I am sorry, but I think I will have to go."

"That leaves us another 7 days. Better than nothing. Perhaps I can join you in London? Let's see what Alan says to this change of plans. It might work out for both of us. I hate to let you go, but I will be busy as well on this end. Let's enjoy the next seven days together and see what happens after that for the time being. Right now, the important thing is we are together. We will have dinner and have an early night. Tomorrow is Casey, and I am sure some work for me with Alan."

"OK, let me get into the kitchen and get started. Check your emails, or whatever you need to do and I will finish up in the kitchen."

Both looked a bit saddened but continued doing what had to be done. Duncan's emails were of no importance. True to form, dinner was indeed ready in 45 minutes. The table had been set, and he was summoned.

"This looks great. I'm sure it will taste great as well. Thanks, Marlee. You are a gem."

Their dinner was interrupted by another call. This time it was Josh Halpern, the DEA agent.

"Hi Duncan. Josh here. How are you?"

"Fine, what's up?"

"I thought you might like to know I am off to Mexico again. Fernandez is already down there. Anything in particular I should know before I go?"

"No Josh, just stay safe. El Guapo is not a nice guy. I am sure he will still be upset at what I did to his car and guest Assisi."

"I imagine that is true, but we are only on an observe and report mission. This time we have a little help from the army in the form of drones and an operator. We plan on watching over his Compound in as much detail as possible."

"That sounds safe enough. But remember, he is very well connected, and if he suspects you two are watching, he may try and take you both out."

"I understand, but D.C. wants more information on what these people are up to, which includes noting everyone that comes in or goes out. One of us is going to be sitting in the same cafe nearby and watching for cars as they leave. The drones will take care of the rest."

"Are you both still staying at the same apartment in Mexico City?"

"Yes we are. The budget will not allow us to use your hotel. Kind of a shame as I liked that place and the rooftop bar."

"That's ok, think of it as a vacation with all expenses paid."

"You do not know our boss a vacation it is not. I have to check in twice a day as does Fernandez. This is not going to be fun. I hope you are enjoying your holiday. After Fort Meade, everyone is a little on edge."

"As am I, Josh. You never know for sure how brazen they will be. Have you heard anything new about our two guests at the fort?"

"They are above my pay grade, so I do not get any information. I do know that the interrogation team is working them both 24/7.

Can't be fun for anyone. Right now, we at the DEA are no longer involved. Ice is probably in on the interrogations, but the team that came wore suits, which makes them a little scary. The base personnel are avoiding their holding area at all costs."

"Probably a good thing. The less you are involved, the less paperwork will be required before this is all said and done. In any case, have a good flight to Mexico and stay out of trouble."

"Thanks, Duncan and enjoy whatever time you have left for vacation. Both Fernandez and I thank you for your efforts to date. Take care, there are a lot of bad guys out there."

"You too, and regards to Fernandez. Keep the faith and stay safe."

They hung up with Duncan going back to his primary interest. Marlee was just finishing up putting everything away from dinner.

"Duncan, how about an early night, all of that walking about has worn me down?"

"Hopefully you are not too tired?" He grinned as he said it.

"I am never too tired where you are concerned. Now let's switch rooms, leave the kitchen."

" Yes ma'am, I am ready and able."

"Marlee had turned down the bed covers. She went to the bathroom and he could hear the shower come on. Nothing like a clean girl, although in her case, he didn't care, as long as she wanted him. She could be covered in ashes and it would not have made a difference. It had been a nice day and tomorrow there was dinner with Casey. Some nerves were active at that thought. When she came out glowing from the hot water, Duncan said it was his turn.

"Don't forget behind your ears lad."

"Will do, now let me get going or we will never be ready."

"I was ready Duncan when we came home. Your phone calls were the problem."

"Sorry about that, but it does pay the bills. Remember tomorrow is Casey for dinner."

" I know, I am looking forward to it. Should I bring pen and paper to take notes?"

"Not funny. I have enough anxiety as it is. You two comparing notes sounds like torture to me."

With that, a few giggles, and they were back in their favorite positions. Marlee stroked his chest and thought yet again how easy this could be to get used to in the future. The question remained, what would that future be for both of them? Cape Town seemed light years away. She understood that Duncan still had to work, but she was jealous of his time and attention. Would that jealousy ever go away? His attention soon made her forget that line of thought. Duncan, as the song said, had slow hands and was rarely in rush. The morning was slow. Breakfast, a quick run with Duncan to the park and then back to the condo.

"That was fun. Not sure I want to run every day in this traffic, but today was o.k.."

"Agreed. The drivers here are a hazard. Sometimes I think they went to a special school to learn how to ignore stop signs, traffic lights, and white lines on the road. It is a skill."

"Makes for a heart pounding run. Not quite how cardio works should be done. It is a wonder there are not more accidents daily. Cape Town is not much better, but we do not have the traffic."

"Yes, I ran from your Flat to Camps Bay many times with little problems. That run here would require hospitalization at best."

"Well, we are back home now. Let's enjoy the afternoon and then Casey tonight. I probably should clean up here a bit and maybe do the sheets."

"Not necessary. We can do them on Sunday. What about a short trip to the Smithsonian Museum? I am sure you will enjoy that."

"O.K. if you are up to another sightseeing day?"

"I do not really care where we go today as long as it is with you. Since your trip is going to be cut off a bit, let's take the time for ourselves. Work can wait right now." Duncan reached over to Marlee pulling her down onto the sofa where he was sitting. That started, the rest of the afternoon was spent in the bedroom. By 5:00 pm, Marlee started to get cleaned up, showered, brushed her teeth and hair. They would have to leave for dinner soon. The afternoon, like all of the times with Duncan was special. She was not going to be happy to have to leave for London.

"My turn to shower and get ready. We should leave in 30 minutes or so. Casey will be on time as usual, and you look fabulous already."

"Thank you, Duncan. I want to like Casey, and hopefully, she will like me as well."

"No doubt, give me 15 minutes and I will be ready to go."

The Uber driver dropped them off a few minutes before 7 p.m. at La Perla on Pennsylvania. The restaurant was already filling up with patrons. Casey was seated by a side window, again overlooking the street and with a clear eye shot to the front entrance.

"Hi Casey, this is Marlee, and of course Marlee, this is Casey."

"My pleasure Casey. Duncan has spoken highly of you." They shook hands while Duncan pulled out a chair for Marlee to be seated. The two women were smiling at one another.

"It is a pleasure to meet the woman who captured the great Duncan Innes. I never imagined anyone able to do this."

"Not sure who captured whom."

"Marlee, I can see why he was attracted to you, but you would have to be special to hold his attention. Looks would not be enough."

"Thank you, Casey, but we have hit it off. I was hoping for some deep dark secrets tonight about Duncan?" The two women stared at one another, then Casey laughed.

"No real secrets on Duncan. What you see is what you get. His job can get harrowing at times, but he is loyal and very considerate."

"Why did you give him up?"

"That is a long story. However, the last time Duncan and I met, someone was about to take a shot at Duncan on Dupont Circle. Fortunately, I was quicker and got the assailant first. The bad news was she also fired a shot off that hit me. My arm is still a little stiff from that incident. Duncan tends to attract a certain class of people. Still, if you don't mind being shot at, he is a keeper."

The two women frowned as Casey said this. Marlee thought back to the incident in Cape Town, when Duncan was accosted by two men near Sea Point. He had come off that one unscathed, although the assailants were not so lucky.

"I do have some experience here with him. I know his job can be dangerous. But life is dangerous. His life is just a bit more overt." They spent the rest of the evening making Duncan uncomfortable with their chatter. He felt like an amoeba under the microscope as they discussed his life.

"That's enough of making Duncan squirm. He is indeed a keeper." Duncan felt a wave of relief pass over him. This ordeal could have been worse. Dinner was served, and the ladies continued to discuss D.C., its vagaries, and jobs. Casey spoke of being a female policewoman with all of the pitfalls associated with the job. Marlee echoed similar experiences in South Africa for women in the workforce. They, in short, got along quite well. The two women exchanged phone numbers and promised to meet up again before Marlee had to fly to London. They had indeed gotten along very well. They only occasionally made Duncan uncomfortable, but that was acceptable in his eyes. It could have gone far worse. Marlee congratulated Casey on her promotion and wished her well. All three parted smiling.

"You can now breathe again, Duncan. I really liked Casey, even though she obviously still had feelings for you. We will become friends."

"I'm sure Casey felt the same way towards you. And any feelings she may have had are just as good friends. That is all." Duncan reached over and gave Marlee a kiss with real heart in it. The Uber driver was starting off to the Condo address.

'I'm glad you two had a chance to meet."

"Me too Duncan. She is lovely and obviously a good friend. I will look forward to having lunch with her next week. Do not worry, I know she will be kind and not throw you under the bus. After all, she saved you once, very little point in doing anything untoward at this time. Now I want you home and in bed. No more thought of Casey tonight, I want your full attention."

"You have it and always will."

MEXICO

The following days until Marlee had to leave for London went too quickly. They did many of the standard tourist things but really enjoyed the time together in Duncan's condo. She fit into his place as he had fit in Cape Town. No additional news from the President had come in, allowing Duncan to concentrate fully on Marlee. Even Alan had stayed quiet, recognizing Duncan needed some time with Marlee. On the Wednesday she had to leave, Duncan helped her with her bags and they took an Uber to the train station. She had to leave from Dulles to fly to London.

"Call me when you arrive in London. Where are you staying?"

"I am booked into the Kensington Close Hotel off the Kensington High Street. It was the closest to the conference. Safe area, and only walking distance to the meetings. I am sure other participants will also be there."

"I hate to see you go, but I will make it back to South Africa as soon as possible. The job I have to complete now, hopefully, will not take too long. I do know, I will miss you."

"And I you, thank you so much for bringing me over to your world. It was exciting and interesting at the same time. I am already anxious to have you back in Cape Town."

"As soon as possible, Marlee. Now through the security nonsense and if you have any problems call me. I will stay at the airport until I know your plane has left. You never know when there will be delays, cancellations, or other problems. Have a safe flight, I miss you already."

She took one last look as she passed through TSA checks and gave a final wave to be swallowed up by the moving line. The smile again had been breathtaking. Duncan went back to the small coffee shop to wait for the announcement of final boarding. That took about one hour and she was gone. He knew the condo would be a lonely place tonight as he left for the train to D.C. proper. He arrived back at the condo around 7 pm. As he entered, his cell phone began ringing. His heart skipped a beat as he wondered if Marlee had a problem with her flight. But, it was Alan.

"Hi Duncan, sorry to bother you, but would you like to have a drink at the Whale? I am sure Marlee has left for London or?"

"Yes to both questions. She left this afternoon and I can walk over to the Whale now if you like?"

"That works, so you in a few."

Duncan changed clothes to something more in keeping with the yuppies in the bar. The Whale indeed was only ten minutes. As he came through the now crowded entrance, he saw Alan sitting at the bar with an empty stool next to him. Duncan nodded as he caught Alan's eye and headed over to the empty barstool. The noise in the bar precluded any real conversation. His drink appeared from nowhere. Alan had preordered.

"You O.K.?"

" Not very happy right now, but it will pass. Marlee is on a plane now for London. I will miss her."

'I am sure you will. She is quite a catch. Both beautiful and smart. I enjoyed meeting her as did the President. We are both jealous."

"Thanks Alan, but right now, the drink looks good, so cheers!"

"And the President?"

"Yes, he called this morning with an update on our friends at Fort Meade and mentioned how much he enjoyed meeting Marlee."

"President or not, he is still just a man and Marlee makes an impression. How did it go with Casey, by the way? That must have been awkward?"

"Somewhat but they got along quite well. They had lunch yesterday but apparently no problems arose from that meeting. I really need to give Casey a call and thank her for not throwing me under the bus."

"Anything new from the President?"

" Yes, how about stopping by my office in the morning? I really do not want to discuss any of this here."

"Sure, I will be there around ten in the morning if that works for you?"

" Good, I will send a car for you. He will be at your building at 9:30 am."

"Thanks, Alan."

"Now finish up your drink, want another?"

"Good idea. Nothing to rush home for tonight."

They chatted for another thirty minutes and Alan left for his home. Duncan finished his drink and headed out. He wondered what the President told Alan, but knew the Whale was not the place to discuss it. The morning would come soon enough. Marlee would call around two A.M. with her arrival news. Hopefully, she had a nice flight. That meant a short night for Duncan, and a lonely one. True to form, the phone rang at 2:30 am. Marlee had made London and was busily traveling to the Hotel. They had exchanged the expected information and protestations. Duncan tried to hide his disappointment as did Marlee. The Condo seemed empty without her. At least when he got up, he would be going back to work. Alan would keep him busy with all of the transfers he would have found from El Guapo into the United States. Running them down would take some time and concentration. He tried sleeping, although difficult without Marlee next to him. The alarm went off at 7:30 am.

Shower, shave, coffee and O.J. would have to do for breakfast. Alan's car would be on time. The phone rang again.

"Hi Duncan. Catch you at a bad time?"

"No Otto. Just getting ready to start my day. What can I do for you?"

"I just called to update you on the BND investigation in Mexico. As you know, they have been busily monitoring El Guapo. They have reported that a van came into the Compound early today with what looked like a prisoner. A man was trussed up and had a black hood over his head. He was taken inside by two guards"

"Any idea, who this is?"

"Right now, the short answer is no. They also reported that they are aware of two DEA Agents in the area keeping tabs on their quarry. The two gentlemen are not very cautious in their surveillance. Too easy to spot. They do not believe the agents are aware of their surveillance alongside them."

"I am aware of the two agents. They are the ones that helped me bring in the two Iranians now at Fort Meade."

"If the BND knows they are there, I suspect that El Guapo's people know it as well. Not a good thing from what we can tell."

"No, it is not. I am meeting with Alan this morning, so I will pass this along if that is okay with you. Perhaps he can warn them through his channels."

"Fine with me, and a heads up that I will be flying to London for a banking conference tomorrow. Any chance you are coming to this one?"

"Not me, but Marlee will be there. Please watch over her, if possible."

"Absolutely, I look forward to seeing her again."

"I am a bit worried about her and would have preferred to have gone with her."

"I understand, and I will be kind and protective. I will let her know we have spoken."

"Thanks, Otto. She has become very important to me. I am always concerned about her safety."

"Leave it to me. I will let you know if anything comes up. The conference is only a few days then everyone goes back home."

"Thanks again, Otto."

"Glad to help. Let me know what you hear about Mexico. I would like to return the favors to the BND if possible."

"Will do. Have a good time in London. Sorry I'll miss you this time. But next time in Frankfurt we can meet up again. How's the family by the way?"

"All good, thanks. More if I hear anything. Stay safe, Assisi is not to be trifled with at any time."

"Will do, but right now, I have to get going. Talk later." They hung up and Duncan finished up his meager breakfast and headed down to the lobby. Alan's car would be there shortly.

As he arrived at the lobby, Alan's limo pulled up to the curb. His phone rang yet gain.

"Hi Duncan, I just wanted to tell you how much I enjoyed meeting Marlee and having lunch with her. You caught a good one. Do not mess this one up."

"Casey, I know and thanks. She is now in London so safe from me."

"You know that is not what I meant. She did not want to leave but had to for work. Sound familiar?"

"Fair enough. When duty calls, as they say."

"She is lovely and a real catch for you. Treat her well, a keeper so to speak."

"Thanks, Casey and agreed. How is the new job going?"

"Very well, although there is a lot more bureaucracy involved. There is paperwork on top of paperwork. Still, overall, it's going well. How about dinner with Marlee gone?"

"I hope she doesn't mind with you being the ex and all that."

"She won't mind, and she did ask me to keep an eye on you till you are back together here or in Cape Town. She knew you might be a little sad with her gone."

"Dinner sounds great. You pick the spot and I will be there."

"Let's meet at the Whale since you know where it is and decide from there where to go.

7 pm work for you tonight?"

"Yes, see you then."

Alan was his usual self when he arrived at the office.

"Good morning Duncan. Thanks for coming."

" I didn't realize I had a choice."

"You I didn't, but thanks anyway. There are a few new developments.

"The package in front of you is all of the transfers of cash we could find from Mexico to the USA with recipients. Research is still running them down as to who they are and what is their legal status. We think we have them all, but can't be sure. Some transfers may not have used the banking system and relied on cash. That is almost impossible to trace. What we are doing however, is anyone that received a wire transfer from the Guapo group is flagged for any cash deposits in recent months to their accounts. An alert has gone out country wide to all banks and systems to be on the lookout for unusual cash deposits. Of course, every deposit has to be under ten thousand, but above 1000 is flagged. Those reports have started to filter in and are cross-matched to the accounts in your package. I should have more in the coming days for you to look into ASAP. This package, however, should keep you busy for a while."

"Gee thanks, Alan. Anything new on our friends at Fort Meade?"

"Right now, nothing. If I hear anything I will get back to you."

They wrapped up the meeting with Duncan leaving with the files that Alan had supplied. He didn't make it past Alan's secretary's desk when his cell phone went off again."

"Duncan, Josh here. I am in Mexico and have a problem."

"What's up Josh?"

"My partner, Fernandez has been kidnapped. He was picked up by a Black Ford SUV as he left the apartment yesterday. I think El Guapo has him."

"How do you know?"

"The doorman to our building saw a large character accoust Jose outside the entrance. He was then bundled off into the rear of the SUV and off they went. I have called H.Q. and they don't know anything. I am not sure you can do anything, but I thought you should know in light of Fort Meade."

"Thanks, Josh. I will get back to you. Are you still in Mexico City, or?"

"Yes, I am waiting to hear from Jose or the office."

"Let me get back to you Josh. I might be able to find out what is going on."

"I wouldn't have called, but you seem to have more juice than I do. I am worried about Jose."

"Understood. Hang in there, I will call back." Duncan was thinking about the arroyo behind El Guapo's compound. He dialed Otto, now in London. The phone connected and Otto came on the line.

"Hi Duncan. I haven't seen Marlee as yet, but do not worry. Still early for the conference."

"Otto, can you check with your friends at the BND and find out if they have identified the person El Guapo had delivered to his Compound? We are missing a DEA agent down there and I am concerned he might be the unknown delivery."

"Sure. I will call you right back. Give me thirty minutes to get an update." He clicked off. Duncan took the time to start working his way through the package that Alan had supplied. Student's for Palestine, and some group called Hamas Freedom Fighters, kept popping up. Who they are is anyone's guess. The naivete of students was appalling. Typical do-gooders with no idea or background in the Middle East but prepared to protest on terrorists' behalf. The old saw of 'one man's terrorist was another's freedom fighter' reared its head. Duncan had seen firsthand what Hamas was capable of and knew that the attention span of the American population was limited at best. Americans would tire of the daily dose of dead Palestinian children, massive destruction of property and body bags lined up on the desert floor. The Israelis had never mounted a decent P.R. campaign and were now paying for it as public opinion shifted away from them. Hamas was winning, and the Iranian-backed protestors were having an impact on public support. The government had already started to reduce aid to the Israelis in the false belief that that was the general citizenry's wish. Once again a short-sighted solution to the problem was being influenced from the outside. There were a few other transfers to obscure groups that appeared to be financing various protest groups on both coasts. One in particular jumped out at him, a Mr. Eddie Hassoon in San Francisco. Mr. Hassoon was an Iranian living in Portolla Valley. A very affluent area above Palo Alto, but near Stanford University. He was definitely worth looking into. As he was reading the file, another call came though, this time Otto again.

"Duncan, I spoke with the BND people. Your agent may be the one unidentified person brought into the compound last night."

" Thanks Otto, probably so. Is there any intel available on the number of people in the compound, for example, and how many staff like maids? And how many others are known?"

"Let me check, and I will call back."

"Thanks, Otto, I appreciate your help." Otto did in fact call back one hour later with the requested information. There were 5 permanent staff consisting of cooks and maids. Ten additional had been counted as support personnel and guards manning the walls of the Compound and presumably the internal monitoring facilities. Added to that was El Guapo himself and his wife plus two children.

Duncan called Alan and updated him on all of this information. He described Josh Halpern's call and what Otto had related.

"Let me call the President and bring him up to speed on what is going on. I think I know what he will want to do and that involves you going back down to Mexico and supporting Halpern in any effort to get Fernandez back. You and Halpern are the only ones with experience to date on the Compound. Let me put that call in and speak with the Homeland Security people on what they want to do. I will call you back and thanks for the update, Duncan." He hung up and Duncan returned to the information package from Alan, he had been working. Two hours went by which must have seemed like forever to Halpern still waiting on a call back. Again his phone chirped.

"As I thought Duncan, the President trusts you and wants you to go back down to Mexico and see what can be done. Right now, Homeland Security can't do anything. See what you can find out and make a recommendation on what our next move should be. Reassure Halpern that we are looking at this very seriously.'

"O.K. will do, please book me a flight and the same hotel in Mexico City. I will get Josh to pick me up again. Also, while I am gone, take a close look at Eddie Hassoon in California. Bank records, real estate holdings, contacts etc., anything that might paint a bigger picture of who and what he is. I smell a rat here."

"Will do Duncan. I will text you the flight information and hotel booking as soon as possible. Be careful down there. The last trip does not need to be repeated. At least this trip will not be on my budget. The bean counters always question everything we do. I will keep the President informed on what you find. Good luck."

"Thanks, hopefully Fernandez will have found himself home by the time I get there, but, I doubt it. Halpern and Fernandez were just too visible. If you get any other information, let me know. I will contact you after I have met up with Halpern. That should be tomorrow sometime. As far as Hassoon is concerned, the more you can dig up the better. I have a distinct feeling that I shall be meeting up with him soon. At least he doesn't live in L.A., there are quite a few Iranians down there. Not sure about San Francisco."

"I should have information on Hassoon when you get back. We are also trying to track Assisi. I will share more when I have it. Be careful down there; we do not want a repeat of Fort Meade. I will check and see if we have any other assets we can tap into while you are there.

Sorry again for breaking up your vacation with Marlee. Is she enjoying London?"

"She is hopefully. Otto is looking after her on my behalf. I will talk to her later tonight. With the time difference, I should be able to reach her and still get some sleep prior to leaving for Mexico. I'll speak to you later from the airport on my way to the South. Right now I have to meet Casey for a drink at the Whale.'

"Take care Duncan, and stay safe. Say hello to Casey as well, you have all the luck.'"

Duncan decided to call Josh Halpern and tell him he was on the way. The text came in from Alan with flight details as he dialed Halpern.

"Sorry for the late call, Josh. I wanted to bring you up to date. First of all, is there anything new on Jose Fernandez?"

"No, Duncan. Still no word. My office is driving me nuts with the same questions. What have you got for me? Any calvary on the way?"

"The bad news is I am the calvary. I will arrive in Mexico City tomorrow afternoon late, at 5:30 pm. Can you pick me up?"

"Yes, what is the good news, if that was the bad?"

"Anything I can do for you and your partner, I will do. I do have some help locally if needed. I'll explain that when I see you."

"O.K., until tomorrow."

"Good night and try and get some real sleep, Josh. We are going to be very busy."

Duncan then texted Otto in London. 'Please arrange a contact with the BND agents in Mexico. He also gave his hotel information and estimated time of arrival. Hopefully, all was well with you in London and talk soon'. A quick pack of bags, passport, credit cards, and a cred pack stuffed into his backpack. The hotel had excellent laundry services, so a lot of clothes were not needed. The trip shouldn't take more than five days. A good outcome was not guaranteed, but longer than five days meant failure. He doubted Fernandez would survive longer than that in any case. Now everything hung on Otto's connection with the BND and would they be helpful getting Fernandez out of El Guapo's grip. He only had a few minutes, then he had to be at the Whale to meet Casey. The walk was short and he hoped the visit would be short. He needed a night's sleep as well. For the first time since he knew Casey, he beat her to the meeting point. He had just ordered a drink when she came through the main entrance.

"How are you, Casey?"

"I am fine, how are you holding up with Marlee gone?" she seemed genuinely concerned.

"I am fine. I miss her of course, but nothing to be done about that. We both answer to a higher calling, so parting ways was necessary.

'I understand. When we had lunch, we did have a chance to bond as girlfriends. I really liked her. I did ask her what she sees in you however, and the answer was much deeper than I suspected. You have a winner there, so do not screw this one up. She was concerned about your job and your future together. I reassured her that you were loyal to a fault and what was meant to be, will be."

"Thank you, Casey. I do not plan on making a mess of this. But the job is the job, as you know. You can't always plan far into the future in this business. Still, I am glad you both like one another and have become friends."

"So what is the plan now? Are you flying to London?"

"No, I have to go back to Mexico and handle a problem there for Alan, or at least try."

"When do you leave?"

"First thing tomorrow. Should be back in a week or so."

"Dangerous trip?"

" I do not know yet. Hopefully not, but the last trip was supposed to be calm and it turned out differently. While I am gone, would you mind checking in on my Condo? You still have a key; I just want to make sure no pipe leak or other disaster occurs while I am gone. If there are any problems, give Alan a call. He can handle them if needed."

"No problem, I will look in every two days. That should do it."

"Thanks, Casey. I appreciate you being so nice to Marlee—above and beyond. Sorry, but I have to call this session short. I need to get some sleep and prepare while I can. I will now be able to get seven hours straight, a gift. Then it is off to the airport and Mexico, OLE."

"Take care Duncan have a good trip and come back safe if possible. Call me when you are back."

"Will do, you stay safe as well. I owe you one."

He gave her a kiss on the cheek and headed home. It felt odd to leave Casey alone in the bar, but she was a big girl. The walk home felt good, and he looked forward to speaking with Marlee again. No doubt that Otto would look after her in London.

Morning came with rain and cloudiness. No email, or phone calls during his prep time to leave. He had spoken to Marlee in the middle of his night. All was well in London and Otto had called and told her they should have dinner that coming evening. They agreed to meet at the conference and, at the end of the afternoon sessions, head off to dinner. He was relieved that all was well and Otto had connected with Marlee. One less worry as he began his trip back to Mexico. Josh had reconfirmed he would pick Duncan up at the Mexico City Airport. The drive to the D.C. airport was uneventful. Uber once again to the rescue. He arrived with over an hour to spare. Coffee from one of the kiosks would do it. Then the long flight to Texas and a shorter one to Mexico City. He texted his departure to Alan, but no return text. He had copied Casey on the text. She would look after his Condo while he was away. The flight was surprisingly empty. Plenty of leg room for his 6'5" inch frame. The Stewardesses were attentive as usual. All in all, a good flight. The Texas to Mexico City one was similar. As advertised, they landed at 5:30 pm. Once through customs, Duncan headed for the exit door. Josh was waiting curbside with his car.

"Hi Josh, anything new on Jose?"

"No, I am pretty sure El Guapo has him in the Compound. What do we do now?"

"My suggestion is we go in there and get him out."

"Sounds good, but not that easy. It is well guarded."

"I know. I suppose we can't knock on the door and say Avon calling?"

"Probably not Duncan. Any better ideas?" Josh Halpern looked very worried.

" A few, but I want to connect with a few Germans here first. That should happen at the hotel tonight."

"Go check in and I will see you at the Rooftop bar, as last time."

Duncan was welcomed back to the hotel and escorted to his room by a bellhop. Halpern took another elevator to the Rooftop bar. The feeling of deja vue was very real. He made one quick call to Alan saying he had arrived. The Germans would turn up around 8 pm at the bar. At that time they would discuss how to get Fernandez out of the El Guapo Compound. Josh was at the same table they had left weeks ago. A glass of wine was perched next to him. Street noises still carried up to the top floor.

"Anything new Josh?"

"Nothing as yet. Who are we meeting here?"

"Two Gentlemen from the BND of Germany. A kind of security arm of the German government."

"Why would they be involved?"

"The man I had you follow, Assisi has been using the German banking system, as well as ours to fund terrorism. They are interested in whatever Assisi does and whom Assisi connects with at any time. Now there is the Cartel connection which they are also investigating. Since our interests align, they offered to help. All of this through a friend of mine in Germany, who is well connected. And of course, now here they are."

Duncan waved to the two men who entered the bar area. They looked very German. Both headed over to the table.

'Good evening gentlemen. My name is Hans Richter and this is Frederick Dietrich. They all shook hands as Duncan made the introductions. The newcomers sat down next to Duncan and Josh.

"What would you like to drink gentlemen?"

"Two beers, preferably pilsners please." The waiter headed off to fill the orders. Duncan and Josh had reordered their refills.

"Our H.Q. suggested we offer any help we can to you two. Any idea what you want to do from this point?"

"Yes, we want to get into the El Guapo Compound and retrieve our friend Jose Fernandez if at all possible."

"How would you suggest we do that Duncan? This place is highly fortified and at least 10 guards to worry about."

"I understand you have a lot of drone pictures of the facility?"

"We do. How about tomorrow morning? I will drop by, and we will go over the pictures. That will give you an idea of how difficult this is going to be if we try to gain unwelcomed access."

"Does 8 am work for you two? Breakfast on me in the first-floor breakfast room."

'O.K., we will see you then. Let the two of us think over the possible entry points overnight until tomorrow, gentlemen."

"Till tomorrow and thanks for your help."

"Duncan we do not have a lot of time for planning etc.. I do not want to think about what they are doing to Jose right now."

"Agreed, but we do need a plan. What do we know now? The compound has staff and help. I think we can ignore the help. The rest 10 guards are probably ex-military and trained. I would think small arms would be their specialty. Not much call for heavy equipment in their small town. The military and the police seem to avoid the area, based on my intel. The Cartel most likely pays off both groups to stay clear."

"I am sure you are right, but there are only four of us and at least ten of them plus El Guapo himself. I am not sure I can ask you two Germans to play along, but you are all we have."

"Don't worry about us. The BND is here to help with whatever it takes. I am sure in the future you will remember?"

"Yes, we will, and I understand I owe you one or two in your case. But also we do have some advantages. The first is: surprise, and the second is motivation. Our first task will be to try and pull off some of the guards and neutralize them. If we can get two or three under wraps, the rest will be easier and the odds will improve. I think I have an idea of how to do that. Then it is back to Avon calling."

"Surprise can be a two-way street. We are not sure of what their motivations are, nor how well trained. "

"We can assume they're bored to tears. Nothing much ever happens there unless they have a group of illegals waiting on transport. Hans seems to think nothing is going on right now. That could change at a moment's notice. But for now, let's work on the idea that it is only the guards and a few civilian workers there. You have been watching the place, are there any reasons for some of the guards to head out of the place?"

"Yes, one reason. Two of El Guapo's kids are taken to school in town every day by at least three guards. They use two SUV's for that. One has the children and a driver and the other two guards are watching for threats from a second SUV. The same route every day, Past the restaurant where we had stopped when you cold-cocked the big guy who was trying to kill Jose and me. Thanks again."

"Ok, that becomes the priority. Take out the two SUVs, preferably without hurting the children. Neutralize the three guards and we have reduced the opposition to seven, agreed?"

"Agreed, but how do we do that in the middle of town? A lot of people around. What if they are in radio contact with the compound? All hell will break loose."

" If I am right, that is exactly what I want to happen. Panic in the compound. At least three more guards will charge out to support the others. We will have reduced the opposition to four plus El Guapo inside the Compound."

"Sounds good, but we now have 6 guards outside. Also presumably armed and some children."

"The children may be the key. If we can snatch them, we have a bargaining chip with El Guapo if he cares for them. We then do the Avon calling bit with two children as bait. El Guapo will be livid, but I doubt he will risk his children. If he does he still loses. The guards at the gate entrance will also be partially panicked. No way for them to know what is happening. One person at the gate will hardly seem like a threat."

"And whom might that be?"

"Me of course. You will be busy with our two German friends containing the others outside of the Compound. In that case, it is three against 6. The odds are vastly improved."

"How do we keep them busy while you get into the Compound?"

"I am sure that Hans and Frederick will have ideas on how to accomplish that. Let's talk about that tomorrow morning at breakfast. I need to source some supplies tonight. You get some sleep, and hopefully, tomorrow we will have Jose in our hands. Good night. See you at 8 am."

Both Josh and Duncan retired to their rooms for the night. Josh had taken a room at the hotel thinking being closer to Duncan would come in handy.

Duncan got on his cell phone and called Alan followed by Otto. Planning was now underway and he thought he could pull this off. If El Guapo was prepared to fire off RPGs in the USA near a Military base, there was no reason he couldn't do the same in a small Mexican town without the military nearby. The next step was trying to get what he needed in the way of ammo and equipment. Alan would have to scramble some assets to get the material into Mexico City by tomorrow. Everything hinged on the children being taken to school in the morning. It was risky, but there just wasn't enough time to do anything else. Every passing day meant Jose Fernandez was that much closer to dying. Alan was not happy with the idea of firing an RPG in a Mexican city, however, he understood the need. Through the President he would get the necessary supplies Duncan had asked for. A small contingent of our soldiers would leave Fort Sam Houston with the supplies by midnight and arrive on the outskirts of San Mateo Atenco by midday. Duncan received confirmation at 9 am in the morning they were on the way. The soldiers would wait for Duncan to appear and take control of the material. By 8 am, he was up, showered, shaved, and ready to rock and roll. It all reminded him a little of Kandahar a few years earlier. Josh and the two BND agents were already enjoying breakfast as he entered.

"Good morning gentlemen. Trust you all slept well?"

"Danke, and you ?" they asked.

"Let' go over my plan and see what you think. We can't do anything today, but tomorrow morning will work. We need today to get the supplies I have ordered." Duncan described what he wanted to do and how. The necessary equipment and ammo would be in place that afternoon. The two Germans agreed that this was really the only option. But the problem remained how to keep the three and then 6 guards from interfering with the overall plan. Taking the second vehicle out with the RPG made sense. The first with the children could be road-blocked by the two Germans very close to the Pharmacy where Duncan had last seen Assisi. Josh would be responsible for firing the RPG at the second vehicle and taking it out of commission. The roadblock, set up by the two Germans, would stop the children's car. It would not be able to back out as the second vehicle would be on fire and block any retreat. Vehicle one, could not be sure if he would be next. They all agreed the panic would work in their favor. Hans and his partner would retrieve the children, ensure they were not hurt, and wait for the backup guards, who would undoubtedly be on their way. They would use zip ties to incapacitate the first driver. All agreed that vehicle two would not likely have survivors or at least badly injured and out of the fray. The third group of at least three guards created the most concern. Duncan suggested that he be stationed at the coffee shop next to the pharmacy. As vehicle number three came by, he would take it out with the second RPG. Collateral damage was not a concern. Locals would flee inside their shops or homes to avoid the carnage when the

shooting began. Both Germans agreed this would work if and when they connected with the needed supplies. Everything hung on Hans and Fredrick being able to capture the two children. Duncan had no doubt he could take out vehicle three, he had done something similar before. Josh also was confident he could take out vehicle two. His service in Iraq ensured he was capable and ready to deal with an RPG in close quarters. The two Germans both had training in urban counterintelligence and were well-trained, and prepared for their current mission. Once the mission was underway, the children would be in the Germans care, who would retire to the restaurant and wait for Duncan's call. El Guapo did not have unlimited resources.

"Time to leave gentlemen. It will take a few hours to get back to San Mateo Atenco. We have to rendezvous with the supply people outside of town and go from there. I hope you all slept well last night, as I doubt you will get any tonight."

"What's the plan for exfiltration?" Hans looked concerned.

"We will be heading for the north in our two vehicles and try and avoid roadblocks. Josh will drive his car with Frederick and I will be hopefully with Fernandez and Hans in our SUV. Assuming we are all in one piece, we should be in the USA via the US Embassy in Mexico City in about 9 hours at worst. You two will not be known, so you are on your own. Head out separately and go underground for a while. That should about do it. I have marked on the map a meeting point at the US border if needed by you. They will be expecting you. For now, let's get going. Hans and Frederick need to look at their ambush place again, and I want a quick look at the Pharmacy and coffee shop. Remember, the best-laid plans have to account for emergencies. No one is left behind regardless of what happens." All three nodded their heads in agreement.

As they say in the Calvary, mount up. We have to leave now." The two cars left in a small convoy checking from time to time if they were followed. So far so good. No tails. Duncan thought about all the possible things that could go wrong but was satisfied with his ad hoc solution to getting Fernandez back. If everyone played their part, EL Guapo was about to have a bad day. Four hours later they were at the rendezvous point. True to form, Alan had come through. A small contingent of men stood by a large advertising sign at the side of the road just outside of town, as agreed. Formalities were exchanged, supplies placed in Duncan's SUV and the two groups parted company. The soldiers, now out of uniform, would head to Laredo and leave Mexico. They had no idea what was going on but wished Duncan's team good luck. Dropping off the ammo and RPG's in another country did not fall into everyday business. It all fell into the category of don't ask, don't tell. Ours is not to reason why phase. They took off to the north on their way to the border. Duncan's team headed towards town. The rest of the day was spent going over various scenarios on stopping the first car with a road block and then to the restaurant for a late dinner. Each knew the task they were assigned and understood the importance of completing each satisfactorily. Now it was a question of waiting for morning. Get set up in place and let the dice roll. Sleeping in their cars was neither of their first choices. A hotel was out of the question, they did not want to leave a paper trail. The few cars that had passed during the night paid no attention to them. The morning proved to be overcast with a threat of rain. Duncan woke them all up.

"Gentlemen, it's time to get going. I will head to the pharmacy and you three to the stopping point on the corner. We will meet up again at the front of the restaurant. I plan to leave the children with the waitress there. She will keep them safe and possibly earn a large tip from El Guapo on their return. Josh, are you ready to go?"

"All set Duncan." Hans and Frederick both nodded. Duncan went back to his SUV and started to head towards the City center and the coffee shop. The other three trailed behind him and broke off at the junction to their holding point. Everything now depended on the habits of the guards and the school children needs to go to school. Duncan found the same parking spot as the last time and pulled into it. He was effectively hidden from the street as his table was obscured by the SUV. He could not see Josh but knew he would now be in position. A raincoat covered his RPG next to him as the waitress brought him a coffee and an arepa. As he took the first bite, two SUVs passed and made the turn towards Josh. The telltale whoosch of the RPG confirmed Josh had fired. This was followed by an immediate explosion and sound of a car scraping along the road. Probably knocked over by the blast. No additional explosions or sounds reached him, but looking back, he saw another SUV leaving the compound and heading his way. This SUV seemed in a hurry. There were actually four men in it. Duncan aimed his RPG and fired as it came next to him. The crash was immediate and loud. This, coupled with the screaming of the waitress, added to the chaos. Duncan ran towards the Compounds main gate. One of the guards was pointing in his direction at the plume of smoke now rising above the shattered second Vehicle. Duncan took both men out immediately with sharp punches to their solar plexus. Both went down gasping. Two zip ties effectively ended their participation in anything that followed. El Guapo himself and the last guard were now running towards Duncan and the gate. One guard got a shot off in Duncan's direction but was immediately hit by Duncan's hand piece fire. El Guapo himself seemed to think better of it and stood there with his hands in the air.

"Where is Fernandez?"

"Is that why you are here, for the gringo DEA agent?" He had a look of disbelief on his face.

"If you want your children back and possibly spare your own life, less talk and more action. Where is Fernandez?"

EL Guapo pointed to the guard shack at the entrance and started to walk in that direction. Duncan followed. El Guapo opened a side door to the shack, which was actually built into the Compound wall.

"He is here and you can have him. He has just been a pain in the ass so far in any case."

"Jose, are you O.K.?"

"More or less Duncan. I think my jaw is broken from being worked over and I have a broken arm. But otherwise just fine."

Duncan leaned back and with a hay maker dropped El Guapo to the shack floor. His jaw would undoubtedly need dental work. He helped Fernandez get up and out the front door. The two guards were still trussed with the Zip ties. Duncan half-held and led Fernandez to the parked SUV. A small crowd of people were now gathered on the corner with the waitress of the coffee shop. As he turned on to the feeder road, he saw what was left of vehicle two. Vehicle three was also demolished, and it looked like there were no survivors. The insurance company would not be happy. Duncan had created a lot of carnage in this small city, but was good for the auto dealers. Ahead he saw Josh and the two Germans none the worse for wear. Josh felt he had to say something. "I love a plan that comes together without me being shot. The children are with the waitress and I gave her a one hundred dollar bill for her trouble. Now would be a good time to get out of here before the local cops turn up. "

"Agreed, let's go now. They headed for the city limits and looked at the plume of smoke still hanging around the disabled vehicle. An ambulance roared by with lights and sirens, followed by a police van. Neither paid Duncan's SUV or Josh's car any attention. The attack had come off as predicted. A lucky shot in the dark. Now they had to get out of Mexico and Fernandez to medical help. Mexico City was the obvious choice. The embassy would be able to help Fernandez get out of the country. The two Germans would split off and go their separate way with the real appreciation of Duncan. Both cars pulled over and the two Germans took the larger SUV and headed off. Duncan, Josh, and Fernandez continued on to Mexico City. Fernandez groaned a few times from the bouncing and his broken arm but otherwise seemed in good spirits.

"Josh, try and avoid the potholes, it is hard on your partner."

"Will do Duncan. What do we do with you?"

"Drop me off at the hotel, I'll pick up my gear and leave. Take Fernandez to the Embassy, they will be ready for him. I texted my office and told them the plan so you will be expected. I suggest you get out of town quickly. They know who you are and will be looking for you shortly. I would rather not come back to get you out of El Guapo's compound. I must admit, though it was fun. "

"Thanks Duncan. I know if Jose could speak properly through

his broken jaw he would thank you as well." Fernandez looked at Duncan and nodded agreement.

"Good luck Gentlemen. Have a good trip home as I doubt you will be much use here in the future. Once I retrieve my gear at the hotel, I will come to the Embassy and hopefully leave with you two."

"Thanks, Duncan. I owe you a drink at a minimum in D.C. when we get back."

"Agreed, I will look forward to it. I doubt you will be coming back here. El Guapo and his people now know who you are, and they will be on the lookout. A new job is in order. Maybe you will be sent to Bali." They all laughed, with the exception of Fernandez, who looked in pain and grimaced. Their drive to Mexico City went off without a hitch. Duncan was dropped at his hotel and went to his room to collect his gear. A quick check of his email and an update sent to Alan was all he had time for at this moment. The response from Alan was immediate. Have a good trip home and check in once he has arrived. He checked out and took a cab to the Embassy. The gate guard was ready for him. He was ushered into a waiting area in the main building. Fernandez was sitting in a corner, well-bandaged, with Josh next to him. They were all given coffee, some nondescript sandwiches and told they would leave for the airport under diplomatic passes in one hour. A private jet would be waiting for them to be flown to D.C. and home. Alan had come through again.

"Looks like a first-class ride home, gentlemen."

"I am ready to go. I have had enough of Mexico to last a lifetime." Josh didn't look pleased as he said this. Duncan agreed and continued eating his sandwich. Hopefully he would survive it and not be tied to the porcelain princess for hours to come. The mission had come off well, with minimum damage. The opposition could not say the same. El Guapo would not be pleased with their performance. One DEA agent was rescued, a few bad guys were put down, and a new friend at the BND. All in all, a good day's work. Now he needed to call Otto and bring him up to date on all that had occurred. The plan would not have come together without Otto's support. The two Germans had performed very well and deserved credit from their superiors. Otto could ensure that happened. Now they just had to get out of Mexico. The US Border Patrol would be on the lookout for them. Once in the U.S. they would be treated well without having to explain what they were doing in Mexico in the first place. It was nice to have Presidential backing. Both men had indeed been a real asset to the mission and much appreciated.

D.C, Recap, and Portola Valley

"Duncan, I have spoken to the President. Both Josh Halpern and Jose Fernandez made it back to US soil. He is most appreciative of what you have accomplished. He hopes you were not injured in any way down there. Both agents will get letters of Commendation in their Service Jackets. He will also, honor your request forwarding a strong thank you note and commendation to the BND for the two German agents that assisted you. That should take care of that for the time being. So far no blowback from the Mexican government nor their Ambassador here in Washington. It looks like everything is just going to disappear. I would also like to thank you and agree with the President that you did a fine job. The DEA and Homeland Security is in your debt."

"Thanks Alan, but as you like to say, I was just doing my job."

"Josh and Jose are being reassigned as we speak. It will take some time for Fernandez to recover from his jaw surgery and broken arm, but everyone believes he will be okay. Both will be staying for some unforeseeable period in the D.C. office. Now the question is what are you going to do? Come to the office and we can decide next steps."

"I think I have to go out to California and look into Eddie Hassoon. Were you able to get any further info on him?"

"Take his file and have a look at it yourself. The others you flagged are still being investigated. I should have more in about a week."

"Alan, do we know where Assisi is right now?"

"He is in the USA but where is still an open question. The NSA is working on that now."

"We have to find him. He is the key to everything. Ideally, I would like to get him into the Fort Meade interrogation room and let the President's experts have a go. If we can break him, we will have a whole picture of Iran's activities in the United States and what their long-range plans are now."

"We will keep looking. But for now, I agree you should go out to California and take a long look at Eddie Hassoon. When do you want to leave?"

"How about this Friday? Please book me a plane ticket, and hotel near Portola Valley. The last time I was out there, I stayed at the Rosewood Hotel off of Sandhill Road in Menlo Park. It is just outside of Portola Valley and near Palo Alto. It is a good jumping off point for the Bay area and off the beaten path."

"I will have tickets, a rental car in your name, and the hotel info emailed to you this afternoon."

"Thanks, Alan, you'd make a good travel agent."

"It's how I can control my budget. By the way, since your last trip, the President has increased our travel budget allowance. All travel will go through his office, which includes costs. At least the Federal Reserve doesn't have to pay for your car wrecks, hotels, and other travel expenses. They were mounting up. Even the DEA was willing to split some costs with us. Will miracles never cease?"

"I am happy for you Alan. Now let's get back to the job at hand. Let me take this file on Eddie Vand go through it. If anything stands out, I will call you. Otherwise, I will call from Menlo Park.

Once back in the Condo, Duncan put in a call to Marlee and Otto, both still in London. Otto picked up first.

"Hello, Duncan. I understand your trip to Mexico was successful."

"Yes it was, plenty of thanks to the BND. Hopefully, both men will get some kudo's for their efforts."

"They have indeed. Your President's thank you went over quite well. The men are now back in Wiesbaden and enjoying some time off of work. Thank you for arranging the thank you, it is and was appreciated. Now I am one more day in London. I had dinner again last night with Marlee. She has become very popular with the banking sets over here. I can't say I do not understand it, but she is working and often asks how are you?"

"I hope you did not tell her what I was up to in Mexico?"

"No, I did not, but she knew something was afoot. I received a number of phone calls while we were together that mentioned you by name, which she overheard. She has been reassured that all is well with you. "You can thank me later. She is really a delight and cares deeply for you. She should be back in her room in about one hour. The last lecture should be winding up now. We will be having dinner again tonight as it is the last evening here. I believe she is flying home to Cape Town tomorrow."

"Thank you, Otto for looking out for her"

"No thanks please, it was my pleasure. Anytime, although if my wife ever meets her, I doubt she will be happy to seeing me looking after Marlee again."

"I understand. I will try and speak with Marlee shortly. I'm off to California tomorrow. We have a lead on one of Assisi's contacts. I will keep you informed. And, thanks again for the help with the BND. If they had not participated a good man might not be home now. We are all grateful. Enjoy dinner tonight, I am envious. You can pass that comment on. Bye for now."

Duncan gave it another forty-five minutes and called Marlee. They spoke for a half hour. She was enthusiastic about the contacts made at the conference and how great Otto had been. Tomorrow would be a long day for both of them. She had an arduous flight in front of her and Duncan had a long day getting to California, and his hotel. They agreed to speak in two days when she was settled at home. Duncan told her a few things about his trip to the San Francisco area without going into a lot of details. There was little point in worrying her. He did not think RPGs would be in play on this trip. He spent the last few hours of his day reading the Hassoon file. A quick call to Casey thanking her for looking after the Condo and a small dinner courtesy of Uber Eats. The morning brought another Uber driver to take him to the airport for the flight to San Francisco. Again, he traveled very lightly with just a backpack, his cred pack, driver's license, and a few day's change of clothes. His Dopp kit had everything he needed. His special pass got him through security with his Glock 43 in its shoulder holster. They still looked carefully at him, but as everything was in order he was allowed entrance to the main concourse. His sports coat effectively cut off view of his holster. Normally, he would not have taken his weapon with him, but in light of events to date, prudence won out over bravado. Too many people had tried to kill him in the past few weeks. No point in tempting fate by being unarmed. Once he arrived at SFO Airport, Duncan went down to the Hertz counter, signed in, and was given a bay number and a Chevrolet sedan. He took the paperwork to the exit and then headed out toward Sand Hill Road. The junction he needed would be off of El Camino Real a main drag that ran from the city to San Jose. This area was Silicon Valley heaven. Start-ups, HP, and many other high-tech companies lined the streets. Sand Hill Road was no exception. At the top of the hill he arrived at the entrance to the Rosewood hotel. He parked near reception, signed in and went to his room. The library the hotel bar, were filled with the yuppie set. More suits and ties than any Mens Warehouse. A quick drink seemed like a good idea. The bar itself was partially filled, while the lounge area was full. The outside patio also had a number of people sipping glasses of wine and enjoying the view of the Portola Valley hills. Duncan decided tomorrow he would take a first pass by the Hassoon house. According to Alan's file, Hassoon was not married and lived alone. His office was in Palo Alto close to Stanford University. He would have to get a look at the house and the office. Now he had to call and check in.

"Hi, Alan. I am at the hotel in Menlo Park."

"You have a good trip?"

"I did, everything here is in order. Anything new on your end?"

"Yes, Assisi is in the United States. We picked him up at customs, as you know, in D.C. So far he is unaware that he is a person of interest. Checking airline manifests has him flying to San Francisco tonight. I would expect him to turn up around Hassoon's sometime tomorrow morning. The President is tracking him through the NSA, but how far that surveillance reaches is anyone's guess. "

"Well, Alan, if he turns up here, I will know it. I plan on camping out at Hassoon's tomorrow and maybe the next day. I need to get into the house and take a look around. The same will hold true for his office. Everything depends on his level of security at this point. More when I have it."

"Just be careful Duncan. Call me back tomorrow if you find anything. We know from Haddad in Fort Meade that Iran is funding the student protests both directly and clandestinely. Most of the money has gone through intermediaries like Hassoon or El Guapo. The NSA thinks Hassoon may be more than just a conduit at this point."

"Let's see what we can find out while I am here. Anything new from Fort Meade?"

"So far, no. They are still emptying Haddad and Saleem. I'll call you tomorrow night. Be careful Duncan."

"Will do, right now, I am going to get a good night's sleep and see what tomorrow brings."

"The ride down to Eddie Hassoon's place in the morning was simple. He took Sand Hill Road down to Portola Road and found the address on a mail box on the side of the road. The house was barely visible from the road. Lots of trees, mostly pines and a density of foliage that seemed planned rather than random. The driveway up to the house was empty. He could see the garage door from his vantage point. The nearest neighbor was at least 100 yards away. It was now 9 am and no visible activity at the house. As Duncan thought this, the garage door began to open. A dark blue

Mercedes pulled out. One driver and then the door began to close. Duncan ducked down to remain hidden from a casual glance in his direction. The Mercedes pulled past him and continued down the road towards Alpine. Alpine would take the car down into Palo Alto. He assumed that the driver was Eddie Hassoon. Probably gone to work for the day. Duncan decided to pull off the road and head up to the Hassoon house as if he belonged. Too much traffic on the road to remain unnoticed. A Town such as Portola Valley would have frequent police cruisers in the area. Where ever there was great wealth law enforcement tended to be extra vigilant. He got out of his car and went to the front entrance. Knocking and ringing the doorbell did not bring anyone to answer the call. He took a slow walk around the house looking for entry points. The rear patio seemed to offer the least resistance to entry and a full view of the inner area of the house. If someone was home, they would become visible quickly. A few cars passed the driveway entrance below as he came around the garage entrance. All good, no alarm bells had been set off. He would come back tomorrow after Hassoon left for work again. For now, prudence was the better part of valor. Duncan drove towards Alpine Road as well, intending to go down into Palo Alto and look at the office building of Hassoon. He drove past the Parkside Grill which looked like a good spot for dinner and a place to park. From the grill he could walk to Hassoon's house without raising an alarm. For now, a quick ride past the office block of Hassoon would have to do. Then, back to the Parkside Grill, and surveillance would begin. As he passed the office block he noticed Hassoon's Mercedes in the parking lot. There was no point in staying there and waiting for Hasson to go home. The office could be entered at night when no one was about and everything was dark and quiet. It only took ten minutes to get back to the Parkside Grill. The lunch crowd was gradually turning up. The few shops next to the restaurant had limited visitors. Parking was simple and non-obtrusive. Duncan decided he would join the lunch crowd. He could sit at the bar, visible from the parking lot, order a sandwich and not look out of place. Only one other patron was sitting at the bar as he entered. She was over-made up, over-jeweled, and over-dyed. The bartender obviously knew her and was placing a glass of white wine in front of her as he sat.

"What may I bring you sir?"

"A glass of your house white would be great. Also a cup of coffee please and a menu. Thanks"

"Our house white is a Kim Crawford Sauvignon blanc. Our coffee is Peets. Does that work for you?"

"It does indeed and thank you."

"I do believe we have never seen you here before sir?"

"No, you have not. I am looking for a property in the area."

"Well best of luck, I know you will enjoy the food here." Small talk ensued and Duncan ordered a salad with feta cheese. The woman at the bar looked over invitingly a number of times as he worked on the salad. He really did not want to be too remember-able. Duncan's cell phone began to chirp as the woman started to say something.

"Hello. Hi Alan, may I call you back. I am in the middle of lunch. "

The woman tried again.

'Hi sir, my name is Hillary Johnson and I am a realtor in the area. May I give you my card in the event you do not have an agent as yet?"

"Certainly, Ms. Johnson. Right now, though, I am just driving around and familiarizing myself with the area. I will keep your card in the event I see something. Thank you, and have a nice day."

"Sorry about that sir. She is a bit of a stalker around here. Always looking for buyers or sellers. Otherwise, she is harmless."

"No problem bartender. I'm sure I will have to deal with her again in the future."

"Too bad, she just tries too hard. Any man in here at the bar is fair game for her."

"Well, it looks like I dodged a bullet then, metaphorically speak-ing. Have a nice day, I am out of here."

It was short walk back to Hassoons driveway. Duncan made

sure he stayed as close to the side of the road as possible. It was starting to get late in the afternoon. Cars zipped past in a town where the local police set up speed traps every 100 yards or so to catch unwanted speeders. Duncan blended in as a walker by the woods on each side of the road. Close to 5:15 pm, the blue Mercedes pulled into the driveway. He could see Hassoon get out of the car without parking in the garage. Hassoon carried a briefcase, looked around and satisfied went to the front door and entered. How long would he stay or was he planning on coming back out? The questioned answered itself two minutes later. Hassoon came back to his car, looked around and then pulled it into the garage. Once the door was closed it looked like Hassoon was there for the night. Duncan walked back to the Parkside Grill. Evening diners were gathering around the bar. Ms. Johnson was not there tonight. Duncan found an open stool and said hello to the bartender. A few husbands and apparent wives sat in the same bar with him. It was getting a little bit noisy but bearable. People trickle in and out over the next hour. Duncan ordered a steak and ate it at the bar. Simpler than going to a table in the now crowded restaurant. Watching Hassoons house had confirmed that Hassoon lived alone. Tomorrow morning would be soon enough to gain access and go through the place. He finished his meal and headed back to the Rosewood. It was time to check in with Alan in any case and bring him up to date on Hassoon and the now empty house during the day and hear if anything new occurred while Duncan was observing Hassoon's home. He also called South Africa, but Marlee was not answering her phone. Emails were non-existent except for robo-emails on aluminum siding, life insurance and other trivia. Spam was a problem regardless of filters. The morning would bring him back to the Hassoon house. Now it was time for a good night's sleep.

His 7 am wake call got Duncan up and ready for the day. Overnight he had taken a call from Marlee, which was short and sweet. He did miss her. She was exhausted after her trip to Cape Town, but they agreed to speak on the weekend. Yes, he was in California, but did not know for how long. Alans' call was a little different after he had shaved and washed up for the day ahead.

"Duncan, we know that Assisi is in San Francisco now. He arrived this morning, and if he is planning to visit Hassoon, he will make the house around 10:30 a.m. He might also just go to the office. Nothing new from Fort Meade as yet."

"Okay, I am off to Hassoon's house now. I want to be sure he leaves this morning for his office. I will call you later if I find anything."

"Good, stay safe. If Assisi turns up while you are in the house, that could be problematic."

"I will be careful. This is really a sleepy town so there shouldn't be a problem."

The drive back down the hill to Portola Valley was uneventful. He passed the giant cyclotron tunnels on his left. They always looked out of place. An eye sore courtesy of Stanford University. The local police had set up another speed trap which seemed to be a national sport in this area. No one looked at him as he drove past onto Portola Road. A few commuters were driving the other way towards Menlo Park. As he pulled closer to Hassoons driveway, the Mercedes was pulling out onto the road. Undoubtedly off to the office in Palo Alto. The Mercedes again turned towards Alpine road. That should give Duncan a few hours to go through the house, unless of course Assisi turned up. Duncan pulled onto the house driveway and parked in front of the garage. He checked again for anyone home, but no response to his knocking or bell ringing. The house was empty. He walked to the back Patio and pulled his door lock picks out of his jacket. Again he checked for CCTV cameras, but saw none. The patio door could have been opened with a screwdriver. Hardly a secure setting. It took two hours to go through the house. The only out-of-place item he found was an airline ticket for two days' time for New York. Time to get out and take a look at the office tonight. A trip now to the office seemed like a good idea. If Hassoon returned, he did not want to be there for Hassoon's arrival or for Assisi. A second speed check was on Alpine road with a few cars pulled over already. The city Fathers knew how to make money for the town's coffers. Duncan thought about Hassoon's upcoming trip to New York. It now looked like Duncan was going to be going to New York as well. As he arrived at the office block, a car identified as an Uber diver was pulling into the lot. Out stepped Assisi with two bags. He was immediately greeted by Hassoon who had come out of the office to meet Assisi.

"Well Alan, Assisi is here in Palo Alto at Hasson's office. I did go through the house but only found a plane ticket for two days from now for New York City. I will go through his office tonight. Anything new on your end?"

"Fort Meade is not producing anything new except for what we already know. A great deal of frustration here. Any suggestion for Assisi?"

"I think the FBI should pick him up and send him to Fort Meade as well. Perhaps we can get more out of him?"

"I will run that by the President. There are certainly some serious legal questions about such a course of action."

"True but under the anti-terrorism rules, possible. Assisi represents a threat. The President and the FBI would be acting on credible threats of terrorism."

"Let's take a look at what you find in the office of Hassoon and go from there. I will brief the President on where we are, but not much to tell him. Hassoon traveling to New York is not an overt threat."

"Agreed, but we have enough on Assisi to justify a stop and detain."

"Agreed but, go through the office tonight, and let's see what we should do next. Happy hunting Duncan. Stay safe." They hung up and Duncan started the drive back to the Parkside Grill. It was too early for the dinner crowd, and only late lunch people were trickling out of the restaurant. He sat again at the bar, ordered a glass of wine, and set in for the long wait for Hassoon and Assisi to come back to the residence. Thankfully the realtor was not camped out at the bar. He used his smartphone to check for emails. One from Marlee saying she missed him and all was good in Cape Town. Another came from the two Germans of the BND. A thank you note for the commendation and the suggestion, when next in Germany a pub crawl would be in order. He responded with a 'by all means'. Now he would wait for Assisi and Hassoon to return. The sun was setting over the hills to the west of Portola Road when he saw the Mercedes turn into the driveway. Two occupants got out by the garage. Assisi was exactly as he remembered him. They went into the house via the front door. Again Hassoon left the car outside of the now closed garage door. Would they stay the night? He decided to wait a half hour and check that the two were down for the evening. After almost an hour, Duncan left and started back towards Alpine Road and the office block. Speed traps had been removed. They must have collected enough fines for the city. Once in front of the office block, Duncan went to the second-floor entrance to Hassoon's office. No one was moving around. He took his pick set out and began opening the main door. Really child's play, once inside he went to the big office towards the back of the building. The next sound he heard after entering the office was the unmistakable sound of a slide on an automatic loading a round in the chamber. It came from behind him in the doorway.

"Both hands up now." Duncan complied immediately.

"Who are you and why did you break into this office?"

Duncan turned towards the voice.

"I was a visitor this afternoon and left my briefcase here. I wanted it back as I have to fly out of here tonight. I wasn't sure if Mr. Hassoon was here or not. I rang but no response." The speaker was a private security guard.

"From what I could see, you picked the lock. Let me call Mr. Hassoon and he can tell me how to proceed. Is that your briefcase there on the seat?"

"Yes sir, sorry for the trouble." As the guard reached for his cell phone, Duncan took one step towards him. With his right hand Duncan grabbed the automatic at the barrel and used his left hand to slap that hand in the other direction from his right. The gun popped loose into Duncan's hand.

"Now that was a neat trick mister. You have done this before."

"True, and I am sorry to ruin your evening. Hassoon will be pleased to know security is on the job. For now, however, I am going to have to embarrass you further. I will keep the gun, but leave it in the post box outside for you. In the meantime, please give me your cell and get into that closet. I am sure you can break out after a bit. Tell your boss two teenagers with guns took you, prisoner, as they ransacked the office looking for valuables. By the time someone gets here, I will be gone, and your job will be secure. "

"What about the briefcase?"

"Just say the teens took it with them. I hope the rest of your evening is uneventful, good luck."

Duncan left the office and put the gun into the post box as he descended to the ground floor. He felt sorry for the guard. Once in the car, he headed back up Alpine Road to Portola Valley. The guard must have gotten out of the closet quicker than he thought possible as the blue Mercedes passed him going down to Palo Alto as he headed up to Portola Valley and finally to Sand Hill Road for the Rosewood Hotel. That had been a little closer than he thought necessary. Maybe the briefcase would offer some valuable information to have made the break in worthwhile. Once again Assisi would be highly annoyed. He doubted they would buy the guard's story. Once at the Rosewood Hotel, Duncan again went to the Library, which was now only frequented by other hotel guests. He sat at the corner of the bar with a good view of the entrance way. The cocktail waitresses really had nothing to do. Only hotel guests were now sitting on stools at the bar. He needed to get to his room, look into the briefcase and then report in to Alan. He would have preferred to go through the entire office, but that had been negated by the local security guard. Hassoon and Assisi would suspect that there had been a reason for the break-in and not have accepted the guard's explanation of teenagers.

The briefcase had been Assisi's. The same material as the last briefcase but for an envelope with ten thousand dollars in it. Probably traveling money. A ticket to New York with the same date to fly as Hassoons was also there. The Daytimer had the Marriot Saddle Brook, N.J., listed for his arrival date. That would give them easy access into New York City via Route 80 which went past the hotel towards the George Washington Bridge. The Day-Timer was also a contact named Kevin Tanner, with an appointment for the following day after arrival in New York City.

New York City

The bar at the J.W. Marriott at Central Park South for 5 pm was listed. Duncan called Alan, although late, and relayed the information and what had happened at Hassoon's office. Alan would book a flight for the next day to New York and a hotel reservation at the Marriott where Kevin Tanner might be staying. In the meanwhile, it was agreed that Alan should get on the phone in the morning with the President and have Assisi and Hassoon followed once they landed in Newark. Keeping tabs on them until they arrived in the city just made sense. Until they all knew what was going on, there was little point in moving against the pair. They would come to Marriott for their meeting with Tanner. Duncan would be waiting. Then everything changed when Duncan's cell chirped again.

"Duncan, some bad news."

"What is it?"

"You were made in Palo Alto. Apparently, Hassoon had hidden CCTV hook ups in his office. You were captured on one of the feeds. Assisi reviewed the feed with Hassoon and immediately recognized you. That puts you very vulnerable in NYC at the Marriott. You will have to keep a low profile when Assisi arrives."

"How do we know this now?"

"Apparently Assisi and Hassoon arrived just after you left and reviewed the feed. Hassoon called the Palo Alto Police Department and filed a complaint for stealing with them. The NSA keeps tabs on all such filed reports and got back to me with a warning. We will squasch the complaint, but since Hassoon knows now who you are, a new level of danger has arrived. What do you want to do?"

" Nothing has really changed. I would like to get a look at this Kevin Tanner and see where he goes after the meeting. Does the FBI still have Assisi and Hassson on their radar?"

"Yes. Two agents on the same flight and a team in Newark will pick them up and follow into the city. Where are you going to wait for them?"

"It is a crowded bar here, so I will be in a corner with my Scotish Tam on, which may make me harder to spot. I should be able to see them without them seeing me. Let's see what happens. No need to panic just yet. I will call after I see them. The two FBI agents should stay with Assisi and Hassoon, I will tag Tanner."

"Okay, I will let the President know and see if he can get the agents to keep up with Assisi. they still remain a terrorist threat. If I hear anything, I will let you know. As always, stay safe."

Duncan had taken a room at the Marriott and decided to go there, change clothes to jeans a collared shirt, his hat and a sports coat. It was really too late in the day to call South Africa, which would have to wait until late that night. A quick shower and he was ready to go. Assisi would arrive early afternoon tomorrow. Time enough for a quick scotch and light dinner. Then, a full night's sleep was a precaution, as he did not know what would happen with Tanner and if there would be time to sleep once, Tanner arrived. The rooms were as expected. Duncan reviewed the files that Alan had given him and the material he had copied from Assisi's briefcase. Nothing jumped out of any of the contacts he had copied from Assisi. Tanner remained the mystery. After expenses, Duncan still had over nine thousand dollars of Assisi. It was certainly nice of Assisi to have financed the entire trip. With that amount of cash, a dinner at Café Del Arte by Carnegie Hall seemed like a good idea. It was walking distance from the hotel and one of his favorite Italian Restaurants. The bar itself was a little pathetic, but the food made up for the small bar. The pre-theatre crowd was already trickling in. Lincoln Center was nearby, and of course, Broadway with all of its theaters. By eight pm the place would be less crowded and fill up again once the first intermissions started. This restaurant was always a favorite stop when in New York City. He was not disappointed. The food was excellent and this evening not too noisy. Tomorrow would be Assisi, Hassoon and Tanner with whatever they were up to. For tonight, all was quiet. He knew that wouldn't last.

His cell phone went off at 3 am.

"HELLO"

"Hi,Duncan, I thought I would check in and see where you are in the world?"

"Good day, Marlee. I am in New York, currently in bed asleep, so if I sound a little bit groggy it is because I am. Still nice to hear your voice. I still do not sleep as well without you."

"Same here. I saw you called earlier, but I was in meetings all day. Is everything okay with you?"

"I am fine. Hopefully not here more than a few days. Let me call you back tomorrow when I know where and what I will be doing."

They chatted for a few more minutes and Duncan said his goodbyes. Still time for a few more hours of sleep. The day would come soon enough. He decided for Sarabeth's on Central Park North for a great breakfast. Assisi and Hassoon would not arrive until three pm; time enough for a nice breakfast on Assisi. At 7 am, he awoke, showered, and by 7:30 am, on his way to Sarabeth's. The walk was good, but still too early for a lot of foot traffic. Once there, the same question as always, did he have a reservation? His response was "No, just give me one of the empty 50 tables. I don't care which one." After a grimace, he was seated with a menu and a coffee dispenser. A far cry from the friendliness of California. At least New York was consistent. He had stumbled on the sister restaurant in Key West some years earlier and was impressed. The New York one, although much larger, offered an excellent breakfast and brunch on weekends. When he finished, Duncan took a short walk in Central Park and decided to call Marlee before she was asleep for the night. No answer, although disappointing, is to be expected. She was probably in Paarl with Kip and Yvonne. He decided to cut the walk short and head back to the hotel. Time to change and set up shop in the bar to wait for Assisi et al. No emails, no phone calls, all seemed quiet for the time being. No news was good news. The hotel maid was finished with his room. The bed was made, new fresh towels and the obligatory mint on his pillow.

Once in the bar, everything seemed normal again. So much of the job was sitting and waiting for something to happen. His corner set gave him a good overview of the entire area without making his presence obtrusive. If someone carefully looked about, he would be seen; otherwise, he blended in as part of the furniture. The scotch and soda he ordered played an important role of keeping the chair next to him open as if someone was about to return. His cell phone remained quiet, something entirely new. The few patrons that were in the area had been there for awhile and started to sound like it. More came in as the afternoon wore on. The bar itself filled rapidly and the fake bar facing the park also had quite a few guests. At 3;30 pm, Assisi and Hassoon entered. Both looked casually around but failed to notice Duncan. They took a table at the far side of the room well away from Duncan. Shortly after their arrival another guest came in also looked around and then immediately went over to Assisi. Assisi stood, introduced the man to Hasso on who also shook hands with the new comer. All three then sat down and ordered drinks from the passing waiter. A discussion followed, with Assisi accepting an envelope from the newcomer, probably Kevin Tanner. Duncan surmised this was probably money as Assisi' cash was still in Duncan's pocket. Two men came into the bar shortly thereafter and took up an observing position at the center bar area. They looked very FBI. Dark ties, white shirts, navy blue suits. They were saved from immediate recognition by the slew of other yuppies who entered the bar loudly. This was obviously a watering hole for the office buildings nearby, everyone dressed the same. Duncan ordered another drink, which he had placed in front of him. This missing guest remained missing. After a half hour of loud drinkers it appeared that Assisi had enough. He got up and headed out of the bar. One of the men who looked FBI peeled off after him, while the other remained looking at Hassoon and Tanner. When Hassoon stood up to leave the other FBI man followed him out the door. Tanner remained sitting and nursed his drink. After another ten minutes, Tanner pulled out his wallet and signaled to the waiter he wanted to settle the tab. That took about five minutes and Tanner got up to leave. Duncan followed him out to the lobby watching as Tanner walked out onto the street. He turned left heading towards Columbus Circle. Traffic had now increased with commuters heading home. Duncan saw the FBI man standing on the corner. He approached the man standing alone and obviously waiting for someone.

"Good evening, are you two assigned to Assisi and Hassoon?" The man jumped at the unexpected voice, and seeing Duncan, a look of recognition appeared on his face.

"I am indeed. My partner just went off to the parking garage to get our car. You are Innes are you not?"

"I am, sorry to startle you."

"No problem. We were told you might be around, and since there are a few 6 feet five gentlemen in the area, it must be you."

"It is indeed. Where did the two go?"

"We're not sure. They both checked into the Saddle Brook Marriott, so we assume they are getting their car from the same garage as ours and will be heading back there."

"What about the man they were sitting with?"

"He came out, turned around, and went back into the hotel. You may have passed him on the way out."

"I did not see him, but possible. He seemed to be trailing you and then I was distracted by the traffic and missed him doubling back."

"It was not hard to understand. He entered the alley over there, and then, you must have passed, he returned to the hotel. Do you have any idea who he is?"

"I think he is Kevin Tanner. Other than that, I do not know a thing about him. What about you two?"

"All we know is he has something to do with Columbia University. Once we had a name from your D.C. contact we ran a quick check on all Kevin Tanners in New York City. Believe it or not, there are over forty of them. Only one seemed a target and that was based on the Columbia connection. He has an apartment a few blocks from here. Do you want the address?"

"Yes please, I still want to keep an eye on him. You and your partner should have a quiet trip back to the Marriott in New Jersey. Let's exchange cell phone numbers in case anything comes up."

"Sure, by the way, I'm Hank Steele, and my partner is Jerry Adams."

"Thanks, Hank. Good luck with those two. Remember, both are very dangerous. Stay safe."

Duncan returned to the hotel and, using the house phone, asked to be connected to Kevin Tanner's room. He was told that there was no one registered with that name. So Tanner had doubled back and headed out through one of the other access points to the outside. The address of Tanner showed an apartment on West 56th Street near 6th Avenue. Across from his apartment was Chopt, a deli restaurant. Now that Duncan knew what Tanner looked like, he decided to set up shop at the deli. This location gave him an overview of a side entrance and a partial view of the front of Tanner's apartment building. He ordered coffee and a danish type of roll. No chance to eat it as Tanner emerged from the building as soon as he had sat down. He was not alone. A young lady walked with Tanner and they headed towards 6th Avenue. The woman had a backpack with a Columbia University label on the flap. Here, indeed, was a nexus between Iran and the University protests. A quick call to Alan might help. He took two photos of the girl and Tanner to forward to Alan.

"I'm not sure the photos will help, Alan, but the male is Tanner, and the girl looks like a student."

"Thanks, Duncan. I will pass this on to the FBI and see if they have anything on facial recognition for these two."

"Thanks, let me know. The two FBI agents were following Assisi and Hassoon to their hotel in New Jersey. Both seemed competent, but I am not sure they realize how dangerous the pair of Iranians are. This might be a good time to take Assisi into custody before they can get anything going."

"I will check in with the President again and see what he wants to do. The idea of snatching foreign nationals on US soil might not go over well, but I see your point. Call me back later tonight or in the morning for updates."

"Will do. For now, Tanner is in the wind with the girl. I am going to taxi up to Columbia and see if they turn up there."

"Good, stay safe Duncan. By the way I am getting tired of saying that. Need a new line."

Duncan's cab ride was less than twenty minutes. He stopped at the gate in front of the quad where the protestor had camped out in previous weeks. The long-term residue and debris were still there. One of the buildings had also been damaged, whether from the fire truck ladder or students could not be seen. A few students were still milling about, either waiting for late classes or friends. One of the crowd was the young lady with a backpack and without Tanner. She was handing out envelopes to a number of older students. A student with one of the envelopes passed Duncan heading out to the main road by the University entrance. Duncan followed for one block catching up with him as he turned a corner out of sight from the school. Duncan innocently ran into him knocking him to the ground. He reached down with apologies and offered a hand up to the student. As he lifted the student up he reached into the pocket of the man and removed the envelope he had seen stuffed there earlier.

"What the hell are you doing?" the student if one, seemed outraged at the jostling.

"I am sorry young man. I tripped on the crack in the sidewalk and you were in the way. Please accept my apologies." He reached out with his right hand offered to shake.

"Forget it, but be more careful."

Duncan smiled and started to walk away. He hoped the student would not miss the envelope for a few minutes as he headed back to a spot to pick up a cab back to the hotel. No yelling behind him, so for the moment he was safe. A taxi was found immediately and took him back to the Hotel. While driving, Duncan took the envelope out and opened it. There was $1500.00 in cash and a short note. The note said the following weekend the protests should restart at the quad, other instructions to follow. No other message or instructions. The protests were continuing to be financed by Iran. There was no other explanation possible. The $1500 would be enough to augment what had been used from Assisi's earlier contribution. Once back at the hotel, he wandered into the bar area and immediately found Tanner sitting at the same table as previously with Assisi. Tanner sat alone but was evaluating everyone who came into the bar. His eyes stopped on Duncan's and then went back to looking at a piece of paper he had spread out in front of him. The paper was a map of some kind. Duncan took a casual walk past Tanners table but could not see what map was there. Tanner had his arm draped over it and was still checking out people who came into the bar. The same yuppie set was returning from the previous evening. Duncan continued on to the men's room, but no one followed. Once back at his table, he waited to see if anyone turned up to see Tanner. A full hour later the man that Duncan had relieved of his envelope came in and walked straight over to Tanner. The two men sat together and looked at the map. Something was up, but the question was what? Shortly after the envelope man had entered and sat down, a woman came in and joined them. She was significantly younger than either man. Duncan again took pictures of the woman for later passing on to Alan. He did this as he sat nursing his drink. WiFi in modern hotels made everything so much easier. Now it was just a question if Alan could identify them. He had passed both the student and the girl's snapshots on to Alan. The modern cell phone really was his best friend. With zoom capability on the I-phone, he was able to capture close-ups with excellent resolution. No one would have seen him taking the pictures. The cell phone was too small to be obvious to a casual observer. One hour later, Alan called Duncan's cell phone.

"We have identified some of the people in your pictures. Kevin Tanner was certainly the one male, we have seen before. He is a graduate student at Columbia. The girl was an undergrad named Cicely Arnold. She doesn't appear to be of interest. The envelope man, as you describe him is Alfred Johnson. He is a senior at Columbia studying Business administration. He did take part in many of the protests at Columbia. He was photographed multiple times by the NYPD. Does not seem dangerous, but certainly one of the agitators at the University."

"Ok, thanks. I am not going to worry about the girl right now, but I think it is time to pay Kevin Tanner a visit and see what I can find. I am going to wait and see when he goes out and then enter his apartment. I'll let you know if I find anything."

"Be careful, Duncan. Tanner may be more than what he seems."

"I am counting on it. Talk tonight."

With that, Duncan went back over to the Chopt Deli to check out Tanner's apartment building. Nothing happened until 5:30 pm when Tanner walked out alone. He was heading towards the Marriott again. Duncan got up and headed over to the building. Just a few pedestrians in the area, but quiet. No sign of Tanner coming back. He waited for someone to leave the building and used that opportunity to enter and bypass the main entrance key system. Tanner was in Apartment 402 on the fourth floor. Th elevator was empty yond took him to the fourth without anyone questioning him. Once in the hallway, he saw Tanner's apartment was to the left of the elevator bank. He went over to the door, knocked, but no answer. As the hallway was still empty, Duncan took out his pick set and opened Tanner's door. Fortunately, there was no alarm. A half-empty box of pizza rested on the coffee table. The apartment was that of a student. Lots of books and paper lying about and a desk that was covered with notes, maps and lists of random sites in New York City. Duncan took a picture with his cell phone of the list of sites as they did not appear to be the standard tourists stops. They included: the Federal Reserve on Liberty Street, the Israeli Consulate on 2nd Avenue, The Tribeca Synagogue on White Street, Mt Sinai Hospital on Madison, the United Nations Building on East 42n Street and the International Plaza, home of the Israeli Permanent Mission to the United Nations. A real assembly of possible terrorist targets. The picture he sent on to Alan MacDonald. All of the sites were heavily guarded since 9/11. This should cause a headache for D.C. now. At the very least a warning of a possible attack would go out. Next stop would be to see what the President wanted to do about Assisi. Now it was a question of which shoe would drop next for Duncan, Assisi or Tanner? A quick call to the two FBI Agents seemed in order.

"Innes here, who do I have Adams or Steele?"

"Hank, Duncan. Jerry and I are still sitting on Assisi and Hassoon at the Marriott in Saddle Brook New Jersey."

"Hi Hank. Anything happening with these two?"

"Not right now. They went a little while ago to the nearby mall but stayed alone. Now back in the hotel, we think for the night."

"Okay, do me favor please, give me a call if they get on the move again. And be careful they are both dangerous. Thanks fellas. "

With Assisi and Hassoon down for the night, there was little that Duncan could do. He decided on a trip down to the bar at the Marriott again. This time, the yuppies were gone and only hotel guests seemed to be imbibing. No sign of Tanner or the girl. His cell phone chirped at the same time his drink arrived.

"Hello Marlee, nice to hear your voice."

"And yours, I miss you. I have been at Kip's and Yvonne's the last two days but am now back to work. Trying to catch up on all the loose ends from London. Lots of emails and follow-ups to take care of now. Where on earth are you right now?"

"I am in New York City looking at Central Park through the

Hotel Bars windows. Should be here another few days and then have a better idea when I can come back to Cape Town."

"The sooner the better. I miss you."

"It's the job Marlee, do believe that I would rather be there with you."

" I know. I did speak with Casey and she said you were okay, but missed me that was sweet of her."

"Casey is great, but still not you. As soon as I know what the plans are, I will let you know. Talk tomorrow or the next day. Things are getting a little busy here right now."

"Dangerous?"

"Not any more than usual. The worst thing that could happen right now is the waitress forgets to put ice in my drink. I'll call as soon as I can."

"Okay, dear. Remember to come as soon as you can. The wine is in the cooler, and we need to take another road trip to Paarl."

"Will do, and I miss you as well." Now it was time to get back to his room.

Assisi and the Targets

"Hi Allan, I am back in the hotel. I spoke with the two FBI agents who have just put Assisi and Hassoon presumably to bed. Tanner is back in his apartment, and the envelope man is nowhere to be seen. Is there anything new on your end?"

"There is a lot of chatter in the Middle East, and from here on, something big is going to happen. Anticipation is running high in the Arab world. So far all we have is what you found in Tanner's apartment. The seven targets, if that is what they are, they have been alerted to be watchful. The Israelis are already on high alert. They pick up the same chatter we do and stay prepared."

"I am going to stay on Tanner. I'll call if something appears to be happening."

"Okay, good night. I will speak with you tomorrow. By the way, the two in Fort Meade are dry. Nothing new and the interrogators think they are tapped out now. The President and his staff are now trying to figure out what to do with them."

"My suggestion would be to drop them off inside Mexico and have plausible denial that we had anything to do with them. "

"Good idea, I will pass that on, and see what happens. The President is still thinking about what to do with Assisi. Hassoon is easy.

He can be arrested and deported as a foreign agent. There is sufficient proof of his involvement with Iranian-sponsored student
unrest in this country to allow for that. That is not the case with
Assisi. If you think of anything, pass it on."

"Will do, but right now I am more concerned with the seven
threats we identified as possible terror targets." Duncan decided to
call it a night, he would take up an observation position in the
morning by Tanner's. One quick call to Casey, which also turned
up nothing. There seemed nothing more that he could do. With
Casey offline and Marlee on the wrong side of the world, he was in
a state of being totally inert. Maybe tomorrow would bring more to
do other than waiting for someone else to precipitate an action or
anything. Assisi and Hassoon were quiet for the moment. Tanner
represented the best course of action going forward. Maybe a visit
to his apartment might get something going again. If Tanner's
movements remained consistent with the past, he would leave his
apartment around 3:30 in the afternoon. An open confrontation
might be the best course of action now. One good night's sleep yet
again seemed like a good idea. Duncan's alarm went off at 6:30 am,
time for a quick shower, shave and then off to Tanners. The few
blocks there would go quickly. What saved Duncan was the FBI
Agent that had been tailing Assisi and Hassoon. It was Hank Steele
who yelled look out Duncan as he left his hotel room. He looked
up at the agent at the end of the hall in the same moment that he
felt the blade enter the lower quadrant of his right side. The
warning had been enough to allow a slight turn away and put off
his attackers aim but not enough to avoid being stabbed. The
Agent fired his weapon hitting his attacker in the chest and immediately putting him down. Duncan fell to the floor, a combination
of pain and now blood loss. The agent came over, checked on the
now dead attacker and tried to stop the bleeding from Duncan's
lower back.

"Do not move just yet, let's get you an ambulance and some
medical attention. The wound looks nasty, but not pulsing, so I
doubt a major artery has been hit."

"Thanks Hank, I owe you one. A doctor seems like a good idea. The hotel may have one on staff."

"I have already called. He should be here in a minute. How are you doing?"

"I'm not as well as I was two minutes ago, but thanks for the heads-up. Why are you here?"

"My partner Jerry and I followed Assisi back to the city. He was dropped off here. I thought you were maybe awake, so I was coming to your room with that update. Jerry is downstairs having breakfast. He is calling for an ambulance."

"Sorry for the mess here. Tanner must have seen me and sent this clown to take me out. I know Assisi knows I am around. He saw me in Mexico and probably the envelope man described me to him."

"Who is the envelope man?"

"From the look of the guy on the floor, I suspect he is the envelope man."

Duncan went into a description of their previous encounter.

"Assisi is, in all probability, behind the attempted hit. He has tried before, once in D.C. with some specialty assassin and now with the envelope man. El Guapo also knows who I am, and certainly, after we took out most of his guards, they will have a vested interest in my removal."

"You do have some interesting friends. We were told about your Fort Meade fiasco, now this attempted murder in central New York." The elevator chimed, and a man with a stethoscope stepped out together with Jerry Adams, the other FBI agent. The Doctor took a look at the wound and said, "You were lucky, your belt took most of the force of the knife but you did get a gash of about three inches into your back. I do not think any vital organs were hit, but do suggest you go to the hospital and get checked out, a CT at a minimum. An ambulance is on its way as are the police. All such incidents are reportable under New York law. The FBI agents can take care of that. Let me look again at the other person, but I believe he is dead from my preliminary evaluation." The elevator chimed again and two officers in blue approached and checked out the cred packs of the two agents. They then asked for Duncan's I.D. and made notes.

"The victim on the floor here is dead. Two of our detectives, and the forensics people will be here shortly. At that moment, the EMTs arrived and loaded Duncan on to a mobile Guerney for transport to the hospital. He had his cred pack, change of clothes brought out for the ride and cell phone. Steele and Adams would stay behind and deal with New York's finest. Duncan put in a call to D.C. from the ambulance and brought Alan Macdonald up to speed on the attempted murder and its outcome. The hotel carpet would have seen better days. As they left the hall became busier and busier with an assortment of cops and others. Duncan's back was beginning to really hurt. Oftentimes, the shock of a sudden wound mitigated pain, but that would soon wear off, and this was no exception.

"What the hell happened, Duncan?" Alan sounded worried.

"Envelope man, decide to kill me and Agent Steele let out a yell of warning. I was quick enough not to be killed but stabbed nonetheless. Now it is a question of pain and embarrassment that this happened to me. The envelope man was waiting outside my door at the Marriott. He was not lucky. Steele killed him with his first shot. Steele is now answering questions to NYPD at the hotel. You might like to have the director of the FBI put in a call and quench all of this now before it gets too hairy for everyone. See if you can get a debrief from Adams and Steele on what they learned about Assisi in the last two days. I am just a little bit annoyed by Assisi at the moment. We need to take this idiot down before he gets really lucky."

"I will call the President, tell him what is going on, and ask again to bring Assisi and Hassoon to Fort Meade. Meanwhile, get checked out and call me when you are out of the hospital."

"Will do, but right now, I want to bring Assisi into the fold so to speak.'

"I am sure you do but let's wait and see what the President

wants first." The Doctor came back into the E.R. as Duncan hung up the phone.

'Good news, Mr Innes. The CT showed no significant damage, but you need stitches, which I am happy to do and then I suggest a few days off to recover. You will be in pain for a few days, but ibuprofen should be enough to handle that. You are very lucky Mr. Innes, a few inches higher and you would have lost a kidney. Our conversation would be very different. For now, let me get one of the nurses to bring me the suture kit and we can start. A small shot for pain in the wound area should be enough. Be careful for the next couple of weeks so as not to tear open the wound, no heavy lifting or sudden movements. I will also give you a ten-day course of antibiotics and pain pills. Be sure and do the complete ten days. We do not want an infection, please. "

"Yes Doc, and thanks. Can you prepare the discharge paperwork so I can get back to my hotel room?"

"I will do that. Give me about thirty minutes. Be careful, Mr. Innes. Please stop being mugged."

"I will try Doc. Thanks again. "

Jerry Adams of the FBI was waiting in the hall as Duncan was discharged.

"Sorry we weren't a little earlier, but it took time to park."

"No problem; Hank was early enough to prevent me from being killed. "

"Right now he is completing the interview phase with the NYPD. Where should I take you?"

"How about we go back to the hotel and my room? The police should be finished when we get back. I need to make some calls and report to my boss."

"Ok, let's go."

The hotel had already replaced the blood-stained carpet, which was very efficient. Duncan went into his room, checked that everything was there, and then started with his calls. The first one was to Alan to update him on his status.

"I'm back in the hotel. I have quite a few stitches, but otherwise,

I'm okay. Steele and Adams are in the hotel as well. Assisi is in his room here, and they are sitting on him until further instructions arrive from D.C."

'I am glad Duncan you are alright. The Director of the FBI took care of any issues with the NYPD. You will not be bothered by any additional questions or interviews with the police. I understand you made a mess of the hotel carpet, but glad you are okay. It was hard not to leak."

"The carpet has been replaced. Any information on the attacker?"

"Yes, he was a Lebanese national being supported by the Arab Federation under Iran. "

"Who the hell is the Arab Federation?"

"A splinter group of Hezbollah. They operate from Southern Lebanon, which has been of little interest to us until now. We were surprised to find them operating here in the United States. One new group to monitor for the FBI."

" I would rather find out about them without donating blood in the process."

"Understood, and the President sends his best wishes for a speedy recovery."

"Thanks, but for the moment I am taking the rest of the day off."

"No problem. Let Steele or Adams know when you are about to leave the hotel. They are going to act as a backup for you while they sit on Assisi. If you go outside, you will be their first priority."

"Thanks; they have done a lot of work up to now, and their support is much appreciated. I am going to take a short nap and then head down to the bar this afternoon. Right now, I have to give Marlee a call and will probably check in with Casey. More when I have it."

Duncan left a message on Steele's cell phone that he would be in the bar around 4 pm. If anything happened they should call. A short call that was unsatisfying to Casey brought no additional news from D.C. , which left Marlee. It was already late in Cape Town but he reached her at home.

"How are you Duncan"

"Well, beyond missing you, I will live. Some local terrorist decided to knife me, but I survived and he did not. The local cops shot him. I just got a few stitches, but otherwise okay. I am back in the hotel taking a bit of a rest after the hospital visit. Should be ready to go out later this afternoon. How about you is all well?"

'My God, yes. I am concerned about you. Why would anyone knife you?"

"We are still trying to figure that out, but I suspect Assisi had something to do with it."

"Well, be careful, Duncan. You are no good to anyone dead, and in particular to me. I need and want to see you again."

"You will. Right now, I just have to keep up with the pills from the hospital, but otherwise, I am fine. I will try a call again tomorrow but do not worry right now. Things have calmed down for the moment."

" I want you here, Duncan, not halfway around the world. Please, no more knife wounds."

"I will try. Have a good night and dream good thoughts." He hung up and started his nap.

Alan called back before he could actually nod off.

"Duncan, are you awake and can you talk?"

"Yes sir. Go ahead, what do you have?"

"We have identified your envelope man as a Grad student at Columbia computer science program. We have started to take apart his laptop and have found quite a few contacts, mostly students, but Tanner was definitely one of them. With his connection to the Arab Federation, the concern now is some of the contacts may be terrorists getting ready to strike."

"Do we have anything specific?"

"Right now, no, but the same list of possible targets you found at Tanners is on his laptop. Times of maximum numbers of visitors, entrances, and other intel were also there. We are now correlating the contacts to students at Columbia and a few at NYU downtown. So far, none are actually on any watch list. They are all undergrads. A few of them turned up on the school roster of known protesters recently arrested or questioned by the schools. The FBI for the moment is viewing them as misguided idiots. Of course, that is meant as an insult to idiots. They are digging deeper. We also confirmed that Tanner supplied the backpacks and funds along with some food vouchers to these students for their protests. Hopefully that is the end of it, but I do not think so. These kids were kept in separate files by Tanner and looked like an advanced cadre. Possible organizers of the protesters on campus. We are looking carefully at them now. Have you spoken to Steele or Adams today?"

" I was just brought back to the hotel from the hospital by Adams so just midday. Last I heard, Steele was babysitting Assisi. I plan on meeting them both here this afternoon. Is there anything new from the president on Assisi and our next moves?"

"Not for the time being. I'll call you tonight with any updates I have re-Assisi. My gut feeling is we will not be grabbing Assisi at this time. That does not mean you have to remain neutral should you run into him."

"Understood, talk tonight." Duncan still had one hour before meeting Steele and Adams in the hotel bar. No shower until tomorrow, do not want to wet the bandages. The television had the usual drivel on it, regardless of which of the 99 channels he sampled. No wonder Americans had such difficulties with current affairs. All of the news channels had agendas. Some were left-leaning, some right, but none middle of the road. Even the BBC channel for Americans was heavily biased. Right now, the only course of action that made sense was to take Assisi and squeeze him dry. Failing that, then Tanner or Hassoon. That would not fly with the FBI, but since Duncan did not report to any of them, perhaps he could act alone. At 4 pm, he got dressed, changed his shirt to avoid the blood-stained look, and headed down to the bar overlooking the park. The same group of local yuppies were starting to congregate at the bar and the center aisle bar. Adams was already there and waiting. Duncan saw him as soon as he entered. He maneuvered through the crowd to Adams' table and sat.

"How are you feeling Duncan?"

"Not too bad considering. Where is your partner?"

"He went upstairs to check on Assisi and Hassoon."

"How long ago was that?"

"About twenty minutes ago."

"I strongly suggest you go check on him. Assisi does not play nice. If he was made by them, they will look for him."

"Ok, I will do that. I'll be right back." Adams got up and left through the same door Duncan used to arrive. At that moment, a contingent of NYPD officers entered through the main doors, heading after Adams. Duncan's drink arrived. An ambulance like the one he had used also pulled up, and two EMTs with Guerney entered the Lobby. There was quite a commotion in the lobby for some time prior to Adams returning.

"You were right. Steele is dead. He was found on the fourth floor by a maid. She alerted the staff who called the cops and the ambulance. It looks like Steele was shot. No sign of Assisi or Hassoon. I checked their room, which was empty. I have to call this in to the FBI, New York office. They will want a team here with the forensics people. Assisi and Hassoon are indeed dangerous. I want these two sons of bitches, asap.

"We should check on Tanner's apartment as well. They may have gone to ground there, but I doubt it. You want to go look, or should I?"

"Duncan, if you are up to it go ahead. Feel free to shoot the bastards on sight. I have to wait for the local team to arrive. I will send backups as soon as they arrive. "

"Ok, I'll meet you back here whenever you can get free. "

"Be careful Duncan. We have used up our allotment of dead Feds at this time." Duncan left through the same doors as the EMTs and headed over to Tanner's apartment. The number of police cars had multiplied over time. The last thing they needed was another Fed mixing into their investigation.

He made it to Tanners in 8 minutes. As one of the occupants was leaving, Duncan used the opportunity to enter the building. There was no one in the lobby, and everything seemed quiet.

The apartment was largely bare. A Columbia backpack was on the bed. What made it unusual were wires poking out of the flaps. There were also a myriad of wires on the bed and some batteries. Wire cutters, plyers and other tools were strewn around the room. He found a receipt from the Columbia Student Bookstore for 8 backpacks like the one on the bed. At first glance, this looked like a suicide bomber assembly area. Seven backpacks were not in the apartment. There was also no sign of Tanner. Duncan immediately called Alan to pass this information.

"It really looks like a bomb factory here. There is no sign of Tanner or the other backpacks he bought. I think we need the FBI's expertise to see if there is any residue from explosives in the room. "

"Agreed, I will call the Director and get a team over there right away. Please wait for their arrival, show them what you have found, and then let them do their thing. I'll check in with you later this afternoon. We do need to track down Assisi, Hassoon and Tanner if possible."

"As soon as the forensics team arrives, I will return to the hotel and reconnect with Jerry Adams. We'll see what the next move should be, but the short answer is that we need to find the other seven missing backpacks."

"Ok, Duncan. Talk to you later."

Within one half hour the forensics team showed up. They immediately deployed their equipment including a portable sniffer for explosives residue. A positive hit for explosives was found almost immediately. The bed had been used as a work bench. The team continued to tear the room apart, removing grills over the heating ducts and looking for anything out of the ordinary. Nothing additional was found. Fingerprints on door knobs were taken and presumably processed via their internet connections. This team came prepared for anything. They rechecked Duncan's credential pack and processed that through their wireless connectors, in short, they were thorough. The entire process took less than one hour. Duncan left and headed back to the hotel and Jerry Adams. He found Adams in the coffee shop making notes in a small pad.

"Hi Jerry, how are you holding up?"

"I am very angry. I want Assisi, Hassoon, and, by default, Tanner as well. Killing Steele is not sitting well. We have a city-wide search going on now. That includes street and traffic cameras. We should pick them up fairly quickly. The entire city is wired, in any case, so the cameras will be hard to avoid. Do you have any ideas?"

" Not for the moment, but my guess is they have gone to ground in a safe house somewhere in the city."

"You are probably right, but we need a lead. Between having you stabbed and killing Steele, these clowns deserve to go down the hard way."

"I agree, but I really want to know what their plan is." Duncan went through a description of what the forensics team found on the first pass. Seven backpacks, potentially bombs, were now somewhere in the city. He also described the sites he had found in Tanner's apartment that looked like targets. The Federal Reserve would be the most difficult to hit as security is very tight. The Israel Consulate on 2nd Avenue would also be relatively well protected. The U.N. itself was always a possibility, as was the Israeli Permanent Mission to the United Nations. The Tribeca Synagogue on White Street and possibly Mt. Sinai Hospital on Madison Avenue, plus many others with an Israeli connection throughout the city, presented themselves as targets.

Adams cell phone went off as Duncan recounted potential targets throughout the city.

"We have one camera that picked up Assisi in Penn station. Our team is looking at that site now. They will call if they get lucky. That is a hard place to pick up anyone that doesn't want to be seen. They could jump a train to anywhere from there and we would be chasing ghosts. No sign of Tanner or Hassoon. We have put out an alert to all of the targets you had originally passed on. They were all told to look for anyone carrying a Columbia backpack. What idiot carries a bomb and self destructs?" Duncan chimed in as Adams hung up his call.

"The people carrying the back packs may not know that is what they are carrying. They may believe they are delivering something as a favor to their assigned destinations. That makes them doubly dangerous. No incentive for self-preservation if they do not know what they are carrying. They walk in, the bomb detonates on a cell signal or a timer, and boom, they have accomplished what they were supposed to do. They look innocuous and are unlikely to be approached by security until they actually try and enter a building. Maximum confusion and a large loss of life at a check point. The desired effect of disruption and chaos has been achieved. If this is going on in multiple locations throughout the city, Assisi et al wins. The news media will play it up big and that means good news for home consumption. Iran will have a large effect for little effort. Our question is how do we stop this?"

"We have to alert as many of the sites we know about as quickly as possible. We know the bomber will be carrying Columbia back-packs. They need to approach with caution to avoid being blown up in the process of checking. Bombs going off throughout the city is a nightmare scenario. I think we should head over to International Plaza and get a first-hand look."

,

"I agree, let's go now. We can get a coffee at Chelsea Bagel shop next door to the Plaza."

"Sounds good to me. How do you know this coffee shop, Duncan?"

"When I first found the list of potential targets or at least what looked like targets I decided to scout them. The bagel shop stood out for its relatively unobstructed view of the Plaza entrance. That is where we should go hang out for the time being. We can get a good overview of anyone passing near by and possibly intercept the back-pack carrier."

'Good, but I am going to call this in and say we are in the area."

"Good idea. Check and see if there is anything new on Assisi. I seriously doubt he will be in the area, but possibly Tanner or Hassoon. As long as we keep a look out for the Backpacker and either man. Extra eyes are a good idea. I suggest we call the Permanent Mission and tell them where we are and that we are also looking. I do not want anyone from the Consulate concerned about who we might be hanging around."

"Good idea. They may be a little trigger-happy if they think there is a bomb threat."

Adams made the calls and Duncan called Alan with an update on what was happening. Assisi, per Adams, had indeed disappeared. Tanner and Hassson were also off the radar. Now, if Duncan was right on targeting, it was a question of wait and see. There was a lot of foot traffic in the area, but as yet no backpackers. They both ordered coffee and Duncan a bagel with cream cheese. After his day he decided he deserved the break. Standing outside and watching the crowds walk buy didn't make eating the bagel any easier, but at least he looked like a natural part of the scenery. It was Adams who noticed the backpacker first coming towards them in the direction of the Plaza.

"Let me grab him, Jerry. I am going to try and maneuver him towards the shop opening. Less damage if he goes off."

"Go ahead Duncan. I will try and block foot traffic coming towards us." Duncan grabbed the young man by the arm and led him toward the door.

"NYPD sir, please come with me. No cause for alarm, just a routine check which occurs from time to time near the Israeli embassy." The young man offered no objection, although he looked a little putout.

"What is this all about officer?"

"Just routine, for your protection and mine. Please remove your backpack and place it on the table here. This will only take a few minutes." The man complied.

"Have a seat over here. Do you have any I.D.?"

"Yes sir." He reached for his wallet and passed his drivers license over to Duncan. His name was Henry Brady. His address was listed in Brooklyn in Dyker Park.

"What is in the backpack sir?"

'I have no idea. I am only acting as a courier. I was paid to deliver it to the Israel mission, leave it behind and go home. You stopped me from finishing the job."

'This may be the luckiest stop you have ever had. Just sit and wait for a few minutes." As Duncan finished his sentence he could hear the arrival of a bomb squad truck outside the shop. They burst into the shop, cleared everyone except Duncan and the courier. One of the officers came over to the backpack and began placing it into a kevlar case. He then asked them both to leave the shop and wait outside. The rest of the shop was now completely empty. Duncan led the young man outside to about 50 feet from the entrance where he saw Jerry Adams conferring with a NYPD officer.

"Young man, you may be transporting a bomb or so we believe."

'That's ridiculous. The backpack is from a friend of mine, Kevin Tanner. We're both graduate students at Columbia."

'When did he give it to you?"

"About thirty minutes go. He had two packs and gave them to other students. We have delivered here before, so I didn't see a problem." At that moment, the front of the shop disappeared in a cloud of dust and debris. The explosion was deafening. Two of the bomb squad raced into the shop looking for their partner.

'Well, young man, you can thank me later for saving your life. That would have gone off on your back sending your head and other body parts to hell and gone. You might want to rethink who your friends are. Kevin Tanner is certainly not one of them."

A small fire became visible through the front of the shop. The bomb squad sprang into action with fire extinguishers. The fire was knocked down as quickly as it began. Jerry grabbed a police officer who emerged from the Plaza and told him to arrest the backpacker and take him down to the precinct for questioning about the bomb that had just exploded. Jerry's cred pack did the trick. The officer marched the man to an arriving police car and both were taken away.

Bad news travels fast. An Israeli security officer appeared at Duncan's side.

"I take it you are Mr. Innes?"

"I am indeed. This is Jerry Adams from the FBI."

'You, called in the threat, thank you. Still not early enough to save this shop or whomever was inside when the bomb went off."

" We tried, but not quick enough. The victim was a bomb squad technician. No one else in the shop and the bomb was not large enough to bring the building down. A lot of shrapnel and ball bearings inside which accounts for all the damage. It was meant to ensure maximum casualties. Probably on a timer. Since I intercepted the bomber, his time of arrival to the plaza was off. That is what saved your security check point but cost this shop everything and the bomb squad tech his life.

"Thank you for that, but I feel for the tech's family and his squad. How did you know for sure who the bomber was?"

'He had a Columbia Backpack which was our target. The man we like for this action is a grad student at Columbia and recruited there. We were looking for the backpack or one of two individuals. The backpack arrived first, so I decided to stop him on the spot and take him into the shop to avoid passers-by. I suspect that the NYPD will find the bomber innocent although stupid. No one in their right mind walks around with a bomb on their backs. He thought he was a paid courier to pick up a little pocket money. So, now of the seven bags out there, we know there are six left."

'Any chance one of the six is still heading here as a backup?"

"Good question, keep an eye out and perhaps one or two of your men to just keep walking around looking. Remember the bag is the marker. I doubt there will be anyone, but caution is warranted." We have to head over to the nearest precinct and check in on our unwitting bomber.

"Thanks again, gentlemen. We will be looking for backpackers."

Both Duncan and Jerry hailed a cab and were taken to the local precinct. They spent two hours with the detective in charge and all came to the same conclusion that Duncan had reached. The bomb carrier might be stupid, but not complicit in the explosion. The police, however, would hold on to the young man for the time being. As they were leaving the Precinct station, Jerry's phone chirped.

"Ok, thanks for the update. I will tell Innes. Talk to you later. "

"What's up Jerry?"

"Two bombs have exploded. One in the subway killing 14 people. The train had been delayed so the timer must have gone off. Both in the same subway car. Quite a mess, NYPD is on the scene with EMTs and a number of ambulances. That leaves four unaccounted for now."

"Since we do not know where these two exploded bombs were intended for, where do you think we should go now?"

"What are our choices?"

Duncan responded with the possibilities he had in mind.

" The Federal Reserve Building, also downtown is the Tribeca Synagogue and The New York Stock Exchange on Wall Street. OK, since the Federal Reserve is mine, why don't you go to the Tribeca Synagogue? Whoever is free first thereafter can go to the Stock Exchange. Just to err on the side of caution, let's call all three by phone with a warning and then head out."

They each departed by cab for their assigned venues.

Duncan reached the Federal Reserve building and took a quick walk around. He noticed immediately the guards patrolling the street and the underground entrance. Before he could react, one guard pulled his weapon and was aiming at a pedestrian walking towards the building. The pedestrian had a backpack securely fastened but looked flustered as the guard yelled at him.

"Get down on the street, lay flat with both hands stretched out so I can see them."

The man complied but looked at a loss for words. As he started to say something, the bomb exploded. The pedestrian's head was launched into the air along with multiple body parts. The guard sustained minor wounds but went down bleeding. Duncan was saved by a parked car which was shredded by ball bearings. He knew the bomber would be identified by the head now lying in the street. The Israelis had learned that suicide bombers almost always blew their heads off and that they could be used for identification. The rest of the bodies would be too mangled to be useful. One more bomb down, three to go. He called Jerry who should have arrived at the Tribeca Synagogue by now. Bringing Jerry up to speed only required two minutes. He heard the bomb go off in the background; now, two to go. Duncan checked on the guard and attempted to stop the bleeding as another guard came out with a First Aid kit.

"No need to help the body in the street amongst other spots, just look after your guard."

Duncan flashed his cred pack which satisfied the newly arrived guard. Who started to bandage various obvious spots on the bleeding guard, but suggested it looked worse than it actually was.

An ambulance arrived shortly thereafter and loaded the injured guard into the rear. They took off, leaving Duncan and the second guard still standing there, looking at the mess in the street. Quite a few cars parked in the area would need new windows, paint, and a good cleaning. Bits and pieces of body would take some time to collect and remove.

"I have to go to another part of the city. NYPD will be here in a few minutes. Are you okay to hold down the Fort? Watch out for anyone with a backpack or you will also be hurt. Here is my card for your records and the security office inside. Your injured partner saved a few lives today. Keep that in mind when you write up your report."

They shook hands and Duncan left for Wall Street. It was not a long walk, but as he walked, he kept scanning for backpacks. Jerry called his cell phone when he was just a few blocks from the Exchange.

"That was close. The bomb went off next to the synagogue. A few broken windows, damaged cars and it looks like three deaths so far. NYPD is here, along with two ambulances and a lot of very unhappy people. The clean-up will be awesome. Blood and guts were all over the street, the building, and the cars.

"Make sure the head is found. It will help with the I.D., and how are you?"

"I was very lucky. A large panel truck was passing between me and the bomber. Remind me to buy furniture from Rooms-to-Go. Their driver was shredded, and their truck looks like a Rent-a-Wreck for trucks. They are going to need a tow truck for this one. The tires are gone. The bomber is in so many pieces, which will make identification difficult. An ink blotter will be needed for the bomber parts. What about you?"

"Basically the same thing, a car saved me. The bomber was dead, and one guard was injured; there were no other victims. '

"Sounds like we were both lucky. Where are you now?"

"I am by the Stock Exchange, but so far no one is here. There are extra police patrolling the area on foot and in squad cars. Our phone warning has worked for now. Still two unaccounted for backpacks. Any suggestions?"

"Before we start running aimlessly around the city, why don't you stay at the Exchange? I want to check in with the Manhattan office and see if they know anything."

"Ok, good luck, call me with any updates."

"Will do, Duncan keep your eye wide open."

'Will do."

Duncan called Alan MacDonald in D.C. and filled him in on all that was happening in New York. The NYPD was claiming the bomb that went off by the International Plaza was actually a gas leak. The idea was to not create panic. The bomb at the Federal Reserve was attributed to a car crash between a Federal Reserve truck and a car driving too fast for conditions. The Tribeca synagogue bomb was an act of local terrorism that was now contained. Anything but the truth. This made the events of the day seem more normal. The events in the subway had not been spun as yet for the media. By tonight there would be an acceptable explanation for the subway bomber and deaths. Alan said he would update the President, but it all could have been worse.

Duncan could not help wondering how being stabbed, almost blown up, and a number of subway deaths was acceptable and could have been worse.

His cell phone chirped the minute he had hung up reporting to Alan.

'We have a lead on Tanner and Hassoon. It appears, however, that Assisi made it through the Port Authority on a bus to New Jersey. CCTV capture of him boarding was noted to late to stop the bus. He is effectively now in the wind."

"Where was the bus heading that he took? "

"Newark airport. We have alerted New Jersey State Cops to look for him and Newark security to apprehend on sight."

"Where is Tanner and Hassoon?"

'Right now, we think that they are holed up on 4th Avenue in Brooklyn. Probably near Methodist Hospital, lots of foot traffic, easy to go undetected. We have two agents in the area now looking. Our techies are looking at CCTV footage of all the traffic and foot cameras in the area. We should know more shortly. You want to take a ride?"

"Sure, pick me up at the east end of Wall Street; we can take the Brooklyn tunnel over there. There are enough police here to stop anyone with a backpack. They are now aware of the danger the backpacks pose. I'll wait for you."

"I'll be there in 15 minutes depending on traffic, got something for you as well."

"See you in a few, then you can tell me what you have for me. If it's Assisi's ass in a sling, I will be happy. Otherwise, nothing would be worth this suspense unless, of course, you are going to let me capture him. Please!"

A few cars passed as Duncan waited. No news, no loud noises, nor falling building parts. No Jerry Adams. So much for just 8 minutes. Losing Steele had been a real fail. Getting stabbed added to that fail. Three bombs going off under his nose did not help his mood. Thinking back to the killings in Germany, London and D.C. made Assisi a prime target going forward. The old fashion 'Wanted Dead or Alive' seemed appropriate. Assisi getting a high-speed exit ticket from this earth seemed very appropriate, if not mandatory. No doubt, Jerry would agree. As he thought this Adams came around the corner and honked once. Duncan hopped in with a, "Hi and let's go!"

"What's the news?"

"We have the last backpack. A local cop found a girl carrying it, but it was a dud, per the bomb squad. It was badly wired, so it didn't go off. They have her at the same Precinct we were previously, but don't expect to get much out of her. She was very lucky."

"You can say that again. Now what other news do you have?"

"It appears we have missed Assisi all together. He was seen at Teterboro Airport in New Jersey. A short time after we picked him up on CCTV, a private jet left Teterboro with a destination on its flight plan to Mexico City. Ten bucks Assisi is on that flight."

"Probably, any chance we can get the plane to land in the USA now?"

"Washington is also looking at that, but so far not enough probable cause on Assisi himself to force a landing."

"Let me call D.C. and see what I can do. I am, however, not hopeful."

Duncan spent the next ten minutes making calls to Alan and the President's number previously given to him. Still no positive result. The private jet would make it to Mexico City.

"Duncan, there is nothing we can do, but both the President and I want Assisi very badly. We have agreed that you should go asap to Mexico City, probably on to El Guapo's compound as the most likely stop-off point for Assisi. You are booked on a government private jet leaving tonight from La Guardia. Right now, get Hassoon and Tanner. Both should then go to Fort Meade asap."

"We are working on it. I'll call back when we have them." As Duncan hung up, Jerry Adams said we have them held up in a deli on the corner. NYPD in the front and rear. No possible exit points for either of them. Let's go get them.

"Jerry, you take the back and I will go in the front. Let's keep the uniforms in place. "

"Take care, Duncan; both are probably armed."

"If you hear a lot of shooting come quickly."

Duncan went through the front deli entrance without a shot being fired. A clerk and female stood behind the counter looking scared. Duncan shrugged his shoulders and mouthed a where?"

Both pointed towards the rear of the store which was cluttered with display racks and refrigeration units. He drew his pistol and started down one of the aisles towards the back. At the end of that row, a ceiling-mounted mirror was fixed. It was pointed at the rear to show the cashier what was going on at the back of the store. In it, he saw Tanner holding a gun and looking at the next aisle to see if anyone was coming. Hassoon was nowhere to be seen. Duncan had as yet not been seen. He kept getting closer to the end of the aisle. Tanner had not turned to look in Duncan's direction. Suddenly Hassoon appeared and yelled to Tanner to watch out for Innes. Tanner turned and was met by Duncan's fist to his jaw. The result was catastrophic. Tanner's jaw was immediately shattered, he dropped his gun and collapsed. Duncan picked up the gun in time to see Hassoon goes for his. Innes fired first dropping Hassoon in a heap on the deli floor. Hassoon was dead, but it couldn't be helped. Jerry Adams burst through the back door, gun drawn, with no one to use it on. He looked disappointed.

"Here is Tanner. He will need dentistry and an ambulance. I am afraid Hassoon is probably dead. He gave me no choice. Still, we will be able to get Tanner to Fort Meade and debrief him completely. Can you take care of that, please? Your director will contact you with the details. "

"Ok Duncan, glad you are good. Where are you going from here?"

"I suspect Mexico is back on my travel schedule. Right now, I have to call my boss and update him and ask him to talk to your Director and get details on the Fort Meade transfer to you. Thanks for the support Jerry, I certainly owe you. Steele would have been proud. "

Duncan spent half an hour on the phone with Alan MacDonald. They agreed on the request for Fort Meade. Alan said he would contact the President and see what they should do next. Undoubtedly a trip to San Mateo Atenco in Mexico was in the offing. The question was what support could be offered by the President. The answer to that question came thirty minutes later.

"I have spoken to the President, Duncan. He has authorized two secret service agents to join you in Mexico as back up. Try not to get anyone killed. They will be on the government jet at LaGuardia when you get there. Check-in on the FBO side of the airport. They will also have some weapons for you, which may be needed. Brief them on what has gone on to date and good hunting. We all want Assisi as quickly as possible."

"Will do, I am going to see if I can get a lift out to LaGuardia. Jerry Adams will be traveling to Fort Meade in an FBI car that is picking him up now.

"I'll call when I know where I will be in Mexico. ""Safe trip, Duncan, and bring back Assisi." Jerry chose that minute to come up to Duncan with Tanner attached by cuffs to Jerry's wrist. He was bleeding from his mouth, which was rapidly changing through all of the colors of the rainbow.

"I need a Doctor for my jaw." He could barely speak coherently.

"Maybe someday we will get you one, but right now, no interest. Suffer on the trip to Washington."

Jerry said his goodbyes and joined another Agent in the waiting car. They were off on the long drive to Fort Mead. Hopefully, they would find every pothole along the way. Duncan felt no pity and with Steele dead, the FBI would have no interest in Tanner's comfort. The next few months would be arduous at best for

Tanner. Now if Duncan could offer the same comfort to Assisi, the whole thing would have been worth it. He decided on a quick call to Otto in Germany.

He was put through to Otto immediately.

"Thanks for taking my call Otto."

"Sure, Duncan, what's up?"

"I am off to Mexico again and probably with a stop at El Guapo's. Does the BND still have any intelligence I can use on El Guapos, compound?"

"I do not know, but will ask and get back to you. Are you going alone?"

"No, I have two agents with me. Should be enough as we decimated his crew the last visit."

Duncan was dropped off at the La Guardia FBO. Two agents at the door immediately stopped Duncan and identified themselves as Secret Service agents. They led him to a tarmac door to a bus that would take them to a small government jet. The portable stairway was up against an open hatch.

"By way of introduction, my name is Harry Carlson, and this is Pete Genzler." They shook hands all around.

"Duncan Innes, gentlemen. A pleasure to meet you. Do you know what we are about to try and do?"

"Unfortunately, yes, we do. A Mr. Assisi of Kuwait is about to be kidnapped in a foreign country by three US Government officials without government sanction or Mexican approval."

"That about sums it up. Mr. Assisi has already killed a number of people, one of our FBI agents, attempted assassination of me twice, and otherwise nasty attempts to bomb various sites in New York City. In short, he is a bad guy. Anything we do to him will just be very minor in the great scheme of things. For my part, tossing him out of this plane from a great height would seem like the least that we can do. How did you two get picked for this assignment?"

"The President asked for volunteers and gave us a broad outline of what we would need to do and who you were. As an added bonus or incentive, I knew Hank Steele very well, I am just a little upset with his killer. We both joined the FBI at the same time and trained together. I was taken out of the program by the Secret Service, but we remained friends." Pete Genzler nodded his agreement with his partner's motivation and said something similar. He had graduated from his FBI class one year after Steele, but knew him. All this fell into the small world category.

"Ok, so you know we are heading to Mexico City and then on to a small town called San Mateo Atenco. Assisi's last stop-off spot was the El Guapo Cartel compound. Hopefully, we will be able to cut him loose from the compound and bring him back to the US. The last time I was there I made a big mess. They may be waiting for us." Duncan gave a description of the activities there and the results.

Harry asked first, "What's the plan?"

"We are going to be ad-libbing for most of the time. I am hoping for some intel before we get there on the ground and then formulate a plan."

"That sounds a bit iffy?"

"You are right Harry. It's all we can do right now. Once I know where El Guapo himself is, we can improvise from there. I suspect he will be away from his compound."

"Who is supplying the intel?"

"I hope to get it from the Germans. They helped in the beginning, which allowed us to retrieve Fernandez, a DEA agent from Guapo's grip. If they still have any assets in Mexico, they will bring us up to speed. If not, we will have to stake out the compound for a few days and see who comes and goes."

The flight passed uneventfully. Duncan gave both agents a history lesson on Iran, including Cyrus the Great, Darius the 1st, and the Ottomans. The connection between Hamas, the Iranians and Assisi rounded off the lesson. A text came into Duncan's phone from Otto: 'El Guapo, not at home , appears to be headed to Bogota with family. An individual looking like Assisi arrived and is currently staying at the Compound. The staff is limited to three servants and five guards. Be careful! They are all ex-military and well-trained. One guard on top of the apartment across the street overlooking the compound. He is assumed to be an early warning system. No help from a local agent is available, sorry. Good hunting."

Duncan filled in the two agents with the text that he received.

"In some ways, this is good news. With El Guapo and family gone, things might be simpler." He described the compound, showed aerial photos from a satellite and what the BND had been able to supply. One main building, two smaller houses, and the guard shack building where Fernandez had been held. There was only one entrance to the compound.

"Since there is only one way in, and that is the front door, that will have to do. One guard is probably in the apartment block across the street, which leaves four others guarding the compound. That, of course, includes the main gate. Our objective will be as follows: Someone had to take out the fifth man across the street. Then the gate guard must be next and we follow through with the other three within the compound. I would like to avoid injuries to any of the servants if possible. Ideally, we go in, take out the guards, and leave with Assisi. Dead or alive works for me. The mandate is, of course, alive, but considering the past, I have no preference. We should not risk any of us to save Assisi. Are we all in agreement?"

The two agents nodded a yes. Duncan immediately sent Alan the request for a truck at the airport and a car at the gas station where he had previously taken out Assisi's limo.

"Now, of course, is the question, what is the magic word to get them to open the gate? Any suggestions?"

"The shortest distance between two points is a straight line. I suggest we crash a rental truck through the front gate. A two-and-a-half-ton vehicle should be enough. That means one of us drives, one jumps out and finishes the gate guard if necessary. We rejoin in the courtyard past the demolished gate. We take the main building first, while one of us remains with the truck and ensures Assisi doesn't slip out past us. The other three guards will have heard the commotion and be coming to see what has happened. We neutralize them asap and move on to a search of the buildings. If we get lucky and find a communication room, let's destroy it on the spot. Hopefully they will have not alerted the local cops. Zip ties for anyone still alive including servants. We regroup and hit the two smaller buildings after the main one. Harry you take the first one on the left and grab Assisi if there. Same m.o. zip ties and frog march him to the truck. Pete you and I will take the other one on the right. Same procedure. No need to be gentle. Who wants to take out the fifth guard in the apartment block?"

Pete responded quickly, "I can handle that. Once we know exactly what floor and apartment should be breached, I suggest I take an afternoon to walk around a bit and see if I can spot him."

"That sounds good. So far, I believe that Assisi will not be armed, but the guards will be. Assisi likes others to do his dirty work. Please be very careful. As soon as possible, we rendezvous back at the truck. Turn that thing around and head out. Assisi goes in the back under a tarp with one of us. We head out of town back towards Mexico City. I am going to have a car stationed at a nearby gas station. We will get rid of the truck and get into the car or SUV. Assisi goes in the trunk. In the event that the compound does reach the cops, they will be looking for the truck, not a car or SUV. That's the best I can do for now. We are all armed now, and should head out to San Mateo Atenco as soon as we pass customs. Let's hope the customs people do not want to inspect our bags. False bottom on one with gear, covered by clothes. I doubt they will bother with X-ray on our bags. The truck and an embassy employee will be waiting outside of baggage claim for us. He has been told we are transporting retail goods to the USA for further sale if questioned.

As promised, an Embassy employee that Duncan had recently met was standing at the baggage carousel.

"Nice to see you again Mr. Innes. Trust you all had a good flight?"

"We did indeed. Thanks for the quick action on your part."

"No worries, the truck is outside. It has an old Goodyear logo on the side. It is also the only size we could get. Two and one half ton."

'That is perfect. What about the car requested?"

"That will be at the gas station with driver as requested. You will swap your truck for his car. In the event that he is stopped, he will have a good excuse for having it. He is repossessing a stolen truck and will have the paperwork for it. The truck was spotted by an employee and he called it in for pickup."

"You have thought of everything. Thanks for all your help. How are you getting back to the embassy now?"

" I will be picked up in a few minutes. Here are the keys."

"Thanks again."

They piled into the truck, it reminded Innes of the 2.5 ton trucks used in Iraq. Easy to drive, but not comfortable. They headed out towards San Mateo Atenco. This truck would not stand out to anyone. It looked like it had been used for many years and smelled like it. Harry drove, Pete in the middle and Duncan took the shotgun position. When they reached Atenco, they parked by the sign where the original equipment to get Fernandez had been held for their arrival. It was a small dirt-holding area but now empty.

"I think I should take a quick walk to town and look around for the 5th guard." Pete got out of the truck and began the trek into the city proper. The walk would only take about thirty minutes, but it gave Pete a chance to get a feel for the place. Mostly dust and a lot of garishly painted houses on the route. As he turned off the main road he could see the Guapo compound off to his left. A guard was standing by the gate and smoking without paying much attention to anyone or anything around him. He looked up and saw a light on the top floor of the apartment house. All the other windows facing the compound were dark. It was now dusk here so people would be coming home shortly. He decided to stop at the café just in front of him. One Cafe Americano should do it. He glanced back towards the Guapo Compound gate and saw the guard flick away his cigarette and casually wave to the apartment block. Looking up allowed him to spot a man hanging out the 4th floor window watching the compound and scanning the road approach. He now knew he had the 5th guard. Pete finished his coffee and headed around the corner by the Pharmacia and then back to the truck.

"Hi guys, we now have the fifth guard in sight. He is on the fourth floor facing the compound. I can get into the building easily as the door to the staircase is open to the street. Just a hop, skip, and a jump to that apartment. It shouldn't take more than five minutes to neutralize him and then down to you at the gate. I suggest we go in the morning light early. The guards in the compound will just be waking up and hopefully sluggish. What do you two think?"

"For my part, nice job and I agree. Harry what about you?"

"No point in delay, it just adds to the possibility that someone else returns unexpectantly."

"Ok, as soon as you have the fifth guard in hand, text a go to us. Harry will begin driving on your signal."

"Works for me. Now, I would like to get at least five hours of sleep. I am glad we bought those Arepas on the way here. I am hungry. I am going to stretch out on the bed of the truck and use the tarp as a mattress. Sleep tight, till tomorrow."

Both Harry and Duncan leaned back in the cab and tried for some sleep. Traffic was very light so they remained undisturbed for the rest of the night. The sun was just starting to peek out behind the hills when Pete left the truck for the apartment house. Harry and Duncan slowly arose from the short sleep, watching Pete head towards town on foot. After a few minutes he disappeared behind some small houses. Ten minutes after he disappeared Duncan's cell phone announced a text message had come in nd was asking for attention. He checked it and saw it was 'All good, fifth guard immobilized.' Duncan responded with good, on our way. The truck started up without a problem, and they rolled towards town. At the right street, they turned left and started to speed up to crash the gate coming up on the left. By the time they reached the entrance driveway the truck was doing thirty miles per hour. More than sufficient for a wooded slatted gate. The guard had come outside probably for another smoke and only saw the approaching truck at the last minute. He managed to jump to the side of the driveway, outside of harms way. The gate itself had no such opportunity and immediately folded into multiple pieces on impact. The majority of what was not splintered was now in the courtyard laying on its side and posing no hindrance to the truck itself. Both Harry and Duncan jumped out of the now stationary truck. Harry took point and watched the main building for the guards that would shortly turn up. Duncan went to the outside guard but was a little late. Pete had already arrived disabled and disarmed the gate guard. He was busily zip-tying the guard up.

"Nice job Pete. What about the fifth man, is he secure?"

"Yes Duncan, he will not be going anywhere for some time. Let's hit the main house." At that moment shots were heard coming from the main building. Harry had managed to pin two guards down behind a porch wall. He was taking the occasional fire from the porch but sporadic. Duncan pointed to the right of the building and sent Pete in that direction. Duncan skirted the truck for a better vantage point.

"Are you all right Harry?"

"No problem, slight scratch on my right shoulder but nothing of import. Where is Pete?"

"He is going to the second building while we take care of these two. What about the third guard. I got him when he started to fire on me. I am pretty sure there are only these two left."

"Ok, see if you can draw their attention and I will try and skirt to the side of the porch on our right."

When Harry opened a fusillade of fire at the porch, Duncan took off for the side of the porch. He kept an eye on both outer buildings as he ran. No takers. He reached the porch second stair case in time to see the last two guards drop their weapons on the floor. The battle was over before it really started going. So much for well trained. Loyalty to El Guapo did not seem to be extended to dying for the cause. Duncan sang out to Harry " They are giving up. Keep an eye on the truck. I am going to ziptie these two and then search the main building. Watch for Assisi I am going in now. Th main hall way had two servants cowering at a corner to another room. Duncan immediately went to them and ziptied them as well. He then proceeded to the kitchen where a woman was hiding in a pantry. She appeared to be the cook. He tied her and then started through the main building. One room he found had communication equipment, but empty. Duncan threw a small grenade onto the table with the gear and left for a lower floor.

The room itself disappeared in a cloud of dust. No one was ever going to use this material again. He passed through the hallway to find Pete and Harry frog marching Assisi onto the truck bed and then covering him with the tarp Pete had used as a blanket.

"Where did you find him?"

"He was just coming out of the shower in Building two. I also have his briefcase, phone and a pile of papers that were lying about his room."

"Nice job Pete, you seem to have handled the brunt of this operation. The President will be pleased he chose well."

"Thanks Duncan, but Harry here kept the guards busy. That made it easy."

'Let's check the truck, make sure it is drivable and get out of here. I am sure the cops will arrive soon."

Harry responded first. " The truck is fine, needs some paint on the front but otherwise good to go. Let's saddle up and leave. Th reversed in the courtyard and left through the demolished gate. Pete was keeping Assisi company as they drove through town. Slow enough not to be noticed but, definitely leaving San Mateo Atenco, hopefully for good. The roads here were good. Duncan had hoped the ride would be uncomfortable for Assisi no such luck. Twenty minutes later they arrived at the gas station. They pulled the truck to the side of the main building. A large brown SUV was standing by them. The driver got out, gave Duncan the keys and started towards the truck. Pete unceremoniously dropped Assisi from the rear while Duncan opened the trunk of the car. Duncan gave the keys to Harry and helped Pete stuff Assisi into the trunk. A small blanket was placed over him to ensure a casual observer would think the back empty. They waved goodbye to the SUV delivery man and watched him leave for Mexico City. Pete sat in the back seat and kept an eye on Assisi. Duncan and Harry discussed the operation and how lucky they really were. Duncan called Alan on his cell phone telling him where they were and heading towards Mexico City and the Embassy for exfiltration. So far a very successful operation. The cops would be looking for a Goodyear truck, not their SUV. The Embasssy would be able to smuggle them out of the country, although Assisi might be a bit uncomfortable in a diplomatic bag. At least that would be unsearchable, and they could be off. Once airborne, Duncan would let Assisi out of the bag. The interrogation and anything else the President had in mind would occur in Washington. Five hours later they were rolling down the runway in a U.S. governmental jet.

Assisi, on being let out of the bag, immediately began complaining.

"You can't do this to me. Mr. Innes, I know you will have me arrested when we land. I am on a diplomatic passport."

"Good luck with that. I'm still debating whether we land or just toss you out of the plane at 10,000 feet and avoid any issues that might arise. Of course, you have experience with that if I recall your efforts in Friedberg, Germany. In this case cement poisoning would not be the issue. We would just drop you over the Gulf and give you the ultimate swimming lesson. You would still hit the water as if it were concrete street. I think medically it is called sudden deceleration syndrome. Fatal none-the-less. Hopefully unpleasant."

"You wouldn't dare."

"Probably not, but these two were friends with the FBI agent you had killed, and certainly, the people on the subway would applaud our efforts. I suggest for the rest of this flight you remain very quiet."

Pete piped up first, "Let me toss him out the door."

" I think we will let Fort Meade have a go at him first. It will be a very long time before anyone hears or sees Mr. Assisi again in our lifetimes." Assisi remained zip-tied to his chair for the rest of the flight. They landed at Andrews Airforce Base where an army helicopter and four M.P.s were waiting to take Assisi into custody. Alan was waiting for Duncan as he deplaned with the two Secret Service agents.

"Gentlemen, this is my boss Alan McDonald."

"Gentlemen, thank you for your efforts and support of our Duncan Innes. I am sure that the President will offer the appropriate thanks etc. Your section will pick you up and take you to your office for a debrief. Duncan, I will give you a ride home and ask or a debrief as well. We meet with the President tomorrow morning at ten. Right now, let me take you home. By the way Casey is there waiting for you. I'll pick you up tomorrow morning at 9 and we can discuss, prior to the President meeting, all that went on in Mexico. Otherwise, get a good nights sleep and take the rest of the day off." They parted company at Duncan's condo. Duncan went via elevator up to his own condo. Old habits die hard, he looked around scanning for threats.

"Hi, Duncan. Just checking on your condo. Marlee had called and said you were not reachable. I should check up on you. Something about a stab wound?"

"Nothing serious Casey. The scar will hardly be noticeable. Just another war story." Duncan gave Casey a full accounting of events in New York City, the death of the FBI agent and his attacker. She did look concerned but seeing Duncan standing before her was a bit of a relief. He did not look to stressed or bruised at all. They chatted for about one hour. Casey made them both coffee and fried some eggs.

"This should refuel you for the time being. You need to call Marlee and say all is good, she is worried."

"Thanks, Casey, I will. I appreciate you being such a good friend."

"After New York, what were you up to?"

He again told the story of Mexico and its connections to the El Guapo cartel, leaving out the Assisi connection. To explain being off the grid, he described a trip to the Central Bank of Mexico and the need for his visit to investigate some fraudulent wire transfers to the USA. Adding some details on how the money ended up with various protest groups around the country, that were now being investigated.

"I can tell there is more to the story, but I will leave it at that."

"There is always more to the story. But, I am ok. The President and Alan are pleased with the results, and that is what counts."

"So, does that mean you have to go back down to Mexico?"

"No, that part of the investigation is now over. I think I will be taking a few months off and visiting South Africa in the near future. Bar anything else happening that should be approved by Alan."

"I should think so. Being stabbed always results in time off. Sometimes permanent time off. I am glad you are okay and also for Marlee's sake. She will be very happy to have you back in Cape Town."

"I'll also be happy to be there. You must come visit when you can. There is something else I want to discuss with you, but it will have to wait until after my meeting with Alan and the President tomorrow. I'll call, and we can have dinner, lunch, or whatever is convenient for you. Even meeting at the Whale would work."

"Anytime, anywhere, Duncan. You know that, now give Marlee a call, she is waiting."

"I will, thanks again for checking on the Condo, until tomorrow." Casey left and Duncan took a quick shower and went through his mail. Multiple new restaurants in the area and a new plumber making himself known. The amount of garbage that accumulated over time was impressive. How much of the Brazilian rainforest ended up in his recycling bin was astonishing.

"Hi, Marlee. All is well on my end, how about you?"

"I have been very worried about you. How is the knife wound?"

"Healing nicely, there will be a small scar, but nothing to get excited about. Sorry I have been off line, but it couldn't be helped. I am back now in D.C. and meeting again with the president tomorrow. Then I should be off. How about I visit for say three months?"

"Oh yes,' she giggled. "I can't wait to have you here again. When will you get here?"

" I'll know tomorrow night and call with my itinerary. Miss you too, but time off is what I need right now, and more importantly I need to be with you again." They continued on with the call for another thirty minutes. Marlee ended it as she needed to get up soon and go to work. Duncan also pleaded tired and decided on an early night. The alarm was set for 5:30 allowing for a morning run, which had been lacking the last days. A half hour should do it, back to the condo, shower, shave and get ready for Alan and the President. 5:30 came quicker than expected, but old habits die hard. Duncan was dressed and on the street with his running shoes fifteen minutes later. Still no visible threats to worry about. The over-achievers were already underway. He passed around Dupont Circle and then back to the condo. By eight he was ready to face the President and Alan. No new emails to worry about. There was a short note from Otto Sternberg in Germany. 'Congratulations on a job well done. He knew about the Assisi capture and the deaths in San Mateo Atenco. He asked for any intel available post-Assisi interrogation. Duncan wrote back, of course. He also mentioned he might pass through Frankfurt on his way to Cape Town. Duncan's cell phone began to demand attention almost immediately post his sent email to Otto.

"Good morning, Duncan. Glad to hear you are going back to Cape Town so soon. If you do fly through Frankfurt, plan on spending one night here and we can catch up. Let me know what you are going to do, so I can arrange a meeting. The head of the BND, Johann Pfaff, would like to meet you as well."

"Sure Otto. I'll call you tomorrow evening or the next day if that works for you?"

"Fine with me. Talk soon, regards to Alan."

"I'll tell him."

As usual, Alan's car pulled up at 9 on the button.

"Good morning, Duncan. You look well rested. Hop in and we're off."

Alan asked for a full recount of the raid on the Compound. They discussed the lack of fall out by the Mexican authorities.

Everything was quiet. No one seems to have missed Assisi. The President was, however, concerned about plausible deniability if needed. That would be a major part of this morning's meeting. It had taken almost a year for the new vice president, nominated by President Evans to be ratified by both houses. The Vice President, Mr. Harland Wilkes would be taking part in the meeting this morning.

"Follow the Presidents lead on the conversation. We do not know what Wiles knows, nor do we think he should know everything that has gone down in Mexico. You still report only to me or the President."

"Understood." Their arrival at the White House was met by the same procedures as in the past. Only this time, it did not go as smoothly as when Marlee came along. They were ushered into the Oval Office and met by the same orderly with the same request: Would they like coffee? Both answered in the affirmative. As it was served, the President entered through his study door.

"Gentlemen, thank you for coming. Duncan, I certainly want to thank you and Alan for all of your help in this Mexico business. You may be pleased to know that Mr. Assisi did not survive the interrogation protocol used. He passed from a massive heart attack. I can't say I am sad at his passing, but we did not get much more information other than what we already knew. The other three are still being worked on. Tanner is starting to show signs of cooperating. He is the lead in this country for all of Iran's activities. He will be a gold mine of information. Sorry you had to be stabbed to get to this point, but you have saved a lot of lives. As far as the dead gentlemen is concerned, no big loss. If there is any blowback, we will deal with that as appropriate."

"Can't say I am sorry to hear he is dead. Now what do we do going forward?"

"That is part of what I wanted to discuss with you, prior to the Vice President joining us. Alan and I both agree that you have been an invaluable asset to the government and the country. The problem is, as an individual you are too visible. My suggestion to Alan is as follows for your consideration. We both agree that you need a corporate veil to protect you and us from the outside world, that being either House or sub-committee appointed to look into the executive branches actions. The short solution is for you to form a security company in Virginia and th US Govrnment contracts with you for activities as yet to be determined. That gives the Federal Reserve and my office the use of your services and a protection for you, as needed. All orders for your services would come in writing and with blanket immunity based on the written order. We would further fund you and your expenses at rate of three million dollars per year. Travel expenses, salaries, e c. To come out of that money. This would effectively remove you from the Federal Reserves budget process and Government Accounting Office Services audit. Your company would fall under the Executive Branch. The stipulation would always be, you report directly to me and Alan. All requests for services would be in writing. The only people who would be aware of your special existence would be Alan, myself, and our in-house accounts. A transfer of the first year's stipend would be one month after forming the new company. Your actions to date and how you are willing to go the extra mile to ensure the success of the mission are appreciated. Further, you would be free to hire or termi-nate anyone you wish. We would review the conditions after every six months to continue as needed. Funding would require one year's notice to terminate this agreement. This protects you and anyone you hire. If we all agree that more money is needed for any given assignment, we meet and establish rules of expenditure to increase funding. Health insurance and retirement would also be included for your employees and yourself once this is established. The Federal Reserve would terminate you as an employee. What do you think?"

" If you do not mind, I need some time to think about this. On the surface it is an appealing proposal. My only concern is the mech-anism for refusing an assignment. That refusal may come about because of potential illegal activity above and beyond what I find acceptable. In short, I can refuse an assignment for any reason, more or less dependent on ethical issues."

"I see no problem with that at this point. I will have a position paper drawn up for you. I know you will be off for the next three months, but thereafter, I want to start this new venture. Is that enough time for you to consider the proposal?"

'Yes sir. It is now August. Let' say the latest I would be able to start is November. If you can get me the drawn up proposal via the Cape Town embassy, I will respond via diplomatic bag with my answer yes or no. I assume that until that decision is made, I will continue to be paid by the Federal Reserve and my expenses covered?"

Alan responded, " Of course, Duncan. We all respect and understand what this all entails going forward, your health insurance continues, and your retirement is now fully vested. This proposal acknowledges just how valuable we believe you are to our country. I strongly urge you not to discuss this with anyone, including Marlee. I wouldn't want to see her compromised in any way. We can discuss this via secure line anytime while you are away."

"Thank you, Alan, and certainly Mr. President. I hope this will not get you into any trouble in the future. I will look forward to receiving your rough proposal. Funding is not my problem, I just hope it will not be one of yours."

'Now.I would like you to meet my V.P. He will not be privy to this, but should be aware of your existence. For now he will only know you are associated as an investigator with the federal Reserve and work for Alan." A button was pressed by the President which immediately resulted in Harland Wilkes entering the office followed by his Chief of Staff.

The president made the introductions.

" I want to congratulate you on your appointment as vice president, Mr. Vice President Wilkes. Both Duncan and I as well as the Federal Reserve wish you very success in this office.

"Thank you both. Hopefully, you will not have to have me terminated as my predecessor. I have been told by the President how much he values you both and your friendship. I hope that will transfer in future over to e as well."

"Certainly sir, but right now we have taken up too much of

President Evans time and should get back to our normal day routine. " It has been pleasure meeting you. Thank you, Mr. President but we must be off. Have a great day." They were escorted by a secret service agent to the car park. His parting words were, "Thank you, Mr. "Innes we are in your debt" So much for secrecy.

"Well, that was unexpected Alan. I will probably accept with the caveats I described. At the very least the blanket 'get out of jail card' needs to accompany each order or mission. For now, I want you to book a flight to Cape Town, via Frankfurt. One day layover in Frankfurt is necessary. I want to catch up with Otto. Whatever we have from the two Iranians and Tanner up to this point has also been promised. I will have to tell him Assisi died, but that shouldn't be a problem. We need their good will going forward and they deserve anything we have for the help in San Mateo Atenco."

"I will get it over to your Condo this afternoon. Thanks Duncan. I think this will be a good deal all the way around. I will also arrange for your flights for tomorrow out of Dulles. I hope you enjoy Cape Town and let's keep in touch. Register with the embassy, so they know how to reach you for the proposal. Your bookings will be emailed to you later this afternoon. Have a good trip. Don't you love politics? At least this new arrangement will keep you invisible on most levels."

"Thanks, Alan. This is all unexpected but understandable. I hope I will not have to pick up the president's dry cleaning as part of the service."

"Not very likely. Just keep away from the politicians."

'Will do. No, drop me off; I will look forward to receiving your email on my travel plans. I would say thanks, but not sure this is a good thing, although it looks good. That is what makes me nervous. What happens if Evans leaves office?"

"He is in office for the next four years, so you are safe for that period. And, I shouldn't say this, but I would hire you back immediately if something changes. That is from one friend to another."

"Thank you, Alan, I appreciate that and trust you. Now I want to get to my condo and pack. I will meet with Otto on this trip."

"Get a good nights sleep. There are two long lights in front of you tomorrow. Say hello to Otto when you see him. I will have everything over to you late this afternoon." Duncan left the car and went to the condo. Th first call was to Casey. Care for a drink at the Whale around 7;30?"

"Sure, see you then. What's up?"

"I'll tell you tonight." He hung up and took another shower. It had been an interesting morning to say the least. There was little possibility he would say no to the President. Now he had to make sure as much as possible was secure in such a deal and he was safe as well as anyone he hired. He was still excited by the idea of seeing Marlee in two days. They had not been apart for very long, but he missed her anyway. The ticket confirmation arrived early afternoon. He would be in Frankfurt at 9 am on Thursday morning. A quick text to Otto and a request for a reservation in Bad Homburg for one night went out. Otto responded almost immediately that he would be picked up at Frankfurt International Baggage Claim. Hotel was booked as well as a dinner reservation at Da Alfonso in Bad Homburg for 8 that evening. Duncan copied the itinerary and texted it to Marlee. His phone rang almost immediately.

"Duncan, I am so happy. Can't wait to see you. I will pick you up at the gate. I'll be the one with the red face of excitement and a massive smile."

"Me too, sans red face. I will call you from Frankfurt, but this trip is definitely on. I miss you and the wine. Alan sends his regards as does the President."

"That is terribly nice of both of them."

"Go back to bed, its too early in the morning for you and you still have to go to work. I am just packing and will have a dink tonight with Casey."

"Please say hello. I really liked her. She must come and visit me here. There is so much I would like to show her."

"I will tell her and see if I can arrange it. Sleep well, see you soon." The chatted for a few more minutes, but Marlee was tired. Both were looking forward to his trip to Cape Town. It was a nice thought that no one was about to shoot, stabbed or otherwise attempt to ruin Duncan's day. It had been a busy few weeks, but for the short term, things would quiet down. Tanner had to be replaced as well as Assisi. Neither would happen quickly. Without proper funding, the student protests would wane. Iran would not give up so easily. Everyone was replaceable. At least now, they knew what to look for and had a short list of organizations to keep a watchful eye on. The president would put the groups identified by Tanner and Assisi records on a watch list. This time, at the first sign of activity, the FBI would step in and detain the instigators.

Now he had to get ready to meet with Casey at the Whale. Sports coat, tie, button down collar would be enough to let him blend in with the locals there. The walk had him looking over his shoulder for threats all the way, but nothing visible. Once in the bar area, Duncan found two stools on the far end with visibility to the front door. Casey swept in at exactly the right time heading immediately over to Duncan's end of the bar.

"I'll have a gin and tonic, please." The barman swung into action. A few of the patrons looked longingly at Casey, which she ignored.

"Still making grand entrance. Nice to see you Casey. How is the new job?"

"OK, but a ridiculous amount of paperwork. If I want to go to the ladies room, I have to submit a request in triplicate and get my bosses approval. I am kidding of course, but you get the idea."

"Welcome to the bureaucracy." He was smiling as he said it.

"Gee thanks, I didn't know it would be so much fun."

"What are you up to?"

"That is what I wanted to talk to you about."

"Go ahead, I am all ears."

"I have had a long talk with Alan and we both think I need to get some distance between myself and the Federal Reserve. There are of course political reasons for this but also accounting issues and plausible deniability."

" Makes sense to me. What are you going to do?"

"For starters, I am going to set up a company 'Cape Security Services. CSS will contract with the Federal Reserve for work I am currently doing anyway. Other assignments may be taken on as they come up. I'll give you details when I am back from South Africa. "

"And, Alan is okay with this?"

"Actually it was his idea. He is concerned with the scrutiny that the federal accounting service may raise. I do a lot off the books, but he is still paying for it and might have to explain just what I do. That would not be good for either of us. You know enough about my activities to see where that might be a problem."

"Agreed, but now what?"

"The new company CSS will operate without direct government scrutiny or oversight. I will still report through Alan what I am doing, but most importantly, not through anyone else."

"Sounds reasonable, but what about your retirement, health insurance, and all the other government perks you enjoy now?"

"They remain the same. In my line of work, retirement seems unlikely, but it is covered by a contract with the Federal Reserve, including health insurance. I have funding for this, covering the next three years."

"That sounds good. When does all of this start?"

"Probably November. "

"It sounds exciting. What do you want from me?"

"I was thinking you could perhaps be a minority partner in this enterprise?"

"How would that look?"

" I would pay you through a CSS a salary of 200k per year and expenses. You would get a car allowance, health insurance, and a funded retirement account based on that salary. You would essentially be running the office and staff and handling the accounting through a new hire to be determined. I trust you, so you would have a lot of autonomy. You might on occasion be the face of the company, when needed. A start date of October is envisaged. No need to agree right now, just think about it for a few days. I'm off to Frankfurt, then Cape Town for three months. If you decide to come on board, you can write your own contract. You will only report to me, and if that is a problem, please let me know. I will never ask you to do anything unethical, but you may be a witness to some unsavory actions that cannot be avoided. In the early stages, there will be a lot of paperwork, like setting up the company, general paperwork, and liaising with Alan. We will need some secure office space. How does all of this sound? You will also be hiring office staff. One secretary to begin with and an accountant."

"On the surface very interesting. I would expect to be kept fully informed on all company activities. That might be a problem for you?"

"Not really. You would need to sign an NDA, but again, I trust you, which is why I am offering this to you."

"Ok, give me a call on the weekend and I will let you know. Giving up the D.C. Police Department and all of its paperwork will keep me from living the dream. Still, working together might be fun and certainly interesting. You do seem to get into all the action that is around."

"Well, have a good night, and I certainly hope your answer will be yes. Do not quit the Police Department if you are going to take the job until I tell you all is complete. As you can image, the contracts need to be completed and money in the bank. That should happen before your start date. It's a lot to ask, but trust me on this. This can only be positive for you and your future."

"Call me on the weekend from wherever you happen to be. Say hello to Marlee for me as well."

"I will do that. I am off to my condo. I need a good night's sleep before I fly tomorrow evening."

Casey left first followed by a lot of male eyes. Duncan left shortly thereafter. As usual, a quick glance around to search for threats of which there were none. Ten minutes later he reached his Condo. Casey would make a great first hire for CSS. Packing was simple and fast. He decided any clothes he might need could be purchased in Cape Town. Two Polo shirts, a sports coat and, one extra pair of slacks, a Dopp kit and underwear, socks should do it. One sweater just in case. He wrote out instructions for the HOA staff. He would leave this at the front office, when he left in the afternoon. His laptop, passport and, Fed Cred pack, cell charger he placed in his backpack in lieu of a briefcase. Duncan travelled light. If it didn't fit in the overhead it didn't go with him. No need for a firearm on this trip so everything was relatively simple. A courier dropped off a thumb drive from Alan as promised. This would be given to Otto. He decided to scan the drive and see if there was anything Otto shouldn't have. All, however, looked in order. He placed the drive in his backpack with his cred pack. TSA and World Traveller Card were also in the bag for his trip and ultimate return. Both would ensure simpler travel through TSA and customs in the USA. The meeting with Johann Pfaff of the BND promised to be interesting. The BND had helped him, so he felt that if they needed anything from him, he would be morally bound to deliver on most requests.

The flight to Frankfurt was uneventful and on time. Once in Frankfurt, as this was Lufthansa, he would deplane in Terminal A. A quick walk past customs with his one carry-on and backpack would see him through arrivals and then the pickup point with Otto. He spotted Otto immediately. A small wave and they shook hands.

"Nice to see you again, Duncan. I'll take you to your hotel, and we'll meet with Pfaff tonight over dinner. If you like, we can stop for coffee in Bad Homburg prior to check-in. Your call."

"Sounds good. I see it's not raining; that is a plus." He smiled as he said it.

"Duncan, do not start. We can stop at the Maritime Hotel and go to their lower level for coffee. It certainly is a pleasure having you back in Germany. Please remember not to hurt anyone while you are here."

"I will try not to hurt anyone. Maybe Herr Peña at the da Alfonso restaurant if the food is not up to par."

"That's fair. Now, bring me up to speed on all that has occurred to you over the last few weeks. How is the knife wound, by the way?"

"Pretty much healed. I am surprised that you know about that."

"The BND told me. They also said you had some fun in San Mateo Atenco recently."

"True, but now over with that part of Mexico. You will not have to look into Assisi any longer, he is no longer with us."

"Pushing up daisies?"

"Yes, but not by my hand. He had a heart attack and failed to recover."

"Thank you for telling me. I can stop flagging any mentions of him in my inbox. Any idea of who his replacement is?"

"Not right now, but we will pick up something if the Iranians continue down this path. I will let you know if anything appears."

"Thanks, Duncan. I am going to go back to my office for a few hours. See you tonight at Da Alfonso's."

"Thanks for the ride and the coffee. See you later tonight. One last thing I should mention: I am going to go independent with a new security company called Cape Security Services. I will contract with the Federal Reserve. That should be running by the end of the year. I will be able to take on other clients on approval of my funding agency, which is also predominantly the Federal Reserve. This is for information purposes only and not widely known. I do not want you to be surprised. I am sure you will hear about it anyhow, but since we are friends. "

"Can I tell Pfaff at the BND?"

"Yes, you may, but it must remain confidential otherwise. I take on clients that are approved by my funding agency and do not compete or are bad for the U.S.government's interest. That must be understood."

"Got it. Good luck with this new venture. Does Marlee know?"

"As yet, no, but it will make sense to her when I explain the reasoning."

"I think I understand. Is this political cover for your activities, or what?"

"You might say that the job remains the same, only a bit broader, and I will be hiring help and have a better logistic support and backup."

"Where will you be based?"

"Still in Washington, I might maintain a small office in Cape Town, as yet to be determined."

"Well, Duncan, good luck. See you tonight with Johann Pfaff."

"I'm looking forward to it. Bye for now." Otto drove away, leaving Duncan in front of his hotel, which was only half a block from the restaurant. Time enough now for a shower and a short power nap prior to the meeting. The die had been cast. Otto's knowing made life easier, and Pfaff would also be an added plus. The BND might, in the future, also be interested in contracting some services. That would be a tightrope to walk in the future. A quick call to Marlee, confirming his flight tomorrow, and then catch up on the time change and get ready for Pfaff. Otto, Duncan and Pfaff sat at a corner round table far away from the' other guests.

'I had wanted to meet you Duncan. Hans Richter and Frederick Dietrick both spoke highly of you on their return to Germany. They, of course, appreciated your thanks and the President's kind words. They will be rewarded, overtime with excellent assignments and hopefully some day we can all work together again. Otto, did tell me of your new venture, and I am sure we will cross paths again in the future. In the meanwhile, I respect the limitations you have placed on any cooperation, recognizing of course that goes both ways."

"Certainly sir."

"Can you give me any more details on our Mr. Assisi and his passing. Perhaps an update on what actually happened in Mexico and then in the USA." Duncan gave a redacted version of events including the bombers in New York and the heart attack that Assisi had suffered. That took about twenty minutes to cover without too many details that could come back and haunt him.

"Very interesting Duncan. In any case, you can count on our support unless of course it would go against our county's interest. I am sure you will maintain contact through Otto here and wish you every success with your new company. That being said, my wife will kill me if I do not get home soon. Thanks for taking the time to meet with me, hopefully we will meet again?"

"I hope so as well sir. Please give Hans Richter and Frederick my best wishes, good night." Pfaff left the restaurant leaving Otto to pay for dinner.

"That went well, Otto. Time will tell if this works for both of us."

'I am sure it will. Enjoy Cape Town and when you are heading back to the USA, please drop by again. I enjoy our meetings and the paid dinners. I have to leave as well. Are you okay with getting to the airport tomorrow on your own, or do I need to arrange transport? Regards to Marlee."

"I'm good. Train to the Central Station and then the airport. No problem. Talk soon and thanks.

Once back in the hotel room, Duncan called Casey. It was early morning in New York, but Casey got up early to work out and get her morning run in, much like Duncan.

" I trust I have not woken you up?"

"Not at 6 in the morning you haven't. Did you get to Frankfurt without getting stabbed or causing any additional mayhem?"

"I have indeed. I had dinner with Otto and his friend. Now I'm planning to get a good night's sleep prior to a very long flight to Cape Town."

"Might I assume you are calling to hear what I think about your proposal?"

"You assume correctly. What do you think?"

"I would like to join you in this venture with a few caveats, one of which is that I can hire and fire office staff, and I have limited paperwork to bog me down. It would be great to leave all of the bureaucratic nonsense here behind. We still need to write up a contract, but in principle, I like the idea. What will Alan say as your funding manager?"

"Like you, it is my call. I believe in the Jesuit School of Management. It is easier to beg forgiveness than to beg for permission." "The details we can work out over the coming week." "Get yourself an EFax account so we can pass a contract back and forth." "I am really happy you want to join CSS." "I know this will be good for both of us." "The details are yet to come, and I will fill you in on the whys and wherefores at our next meeting." "Thanks, Casey; it will be great to work with you." "I will call you next week with a list of things that need to be done. You will have to serve as a gopher while I am away. Start looking around for an office secretary. Office space will also be needed. Say around 3,000 square feet to begin with." "I will come up with a list as soon as possible." "More next week." "In-house staff will be solely your area. All will have to sign an NDA, etc. Now I need to sleep. Long flight tomorrow."

"Have a good night and stay safe, as they say—not that you will listen."

"Gee, thanks, Casey."

The rest of the evening and the next morning were uneventful. Duncan finished packing the last few things he didn't want to leave behind and headed for Frankfurt International Airport. His flight would leave at 10p.m.. and land in Cape Town at 10 a.m. the next day. Marlee would be waiting at baggage claim. A very pleasant thought prior to a long flight. Seven hours later, Duncan was seated on his Cape Town flight. Business class made the trip more acceptable, but still long. His aisle seat was perfect, no passenger at the window next to him. This would be a quiet trip. He pulled out his laptop once airborne and started making lists of needs for the new company. Using Jessica Sierakowski from Broad and Lane as the law firm seemed appropriate. Jessica knew what he did for a living; if not for the details, she would understand the need for discretion. Putting together an LLC or Inc was right up her alley. She also knew Casey so that made the contact easy. Now he just needed to wait for the President's proposal in writing, and it was a go. Another five hours of sleep helped to pass the flight time. As the plane started its descent to Cape Town, he could see out of his window the table-cloth flowing over Table Mountain. It was a view that he never tired of seeing. He felt his heart speed up in anticipation of seeing Marlee again. Walking from the gate to baggage claim went by very quickly. She was indeed waiting by the carousel.

"Hi, beautiful. Truly a sight for sore eyes."

"For me too, Duncan. How was the flight?"

"At this point, who cares? I am back with you; that is what counts. Let me just hold you and smell the gardenias again."

"What, no kiss?" She was smiling.

"Absolutely, but we do not want to embarrass the other passengers."

"Well, let's go home. The car is just outside."

The drive to Disa Park was simple and quick. The view remained magnificent, as did Marlee. They were in her flat by noon.

"Marlee, come over to the sofa. I do not need anything but to hold you for as long as possible. The smell of gardenias was intoxicating. Neither knew for sure when the next trip would come up, but holding one another tightly was enough for now.